The Devil's Garden

For my Mum.

Much loved, and missed every day.

xxx

Also,

In memory of the poor,

unfortunate victims of

the events of Pendle, 1612.

The Devil's Garden

There was a stench in the air. Not the usual, expected natural aroma of the countryside, with the mass of sheep that haunted the hillside and the cattle that grazed in its fields, but a strong, putrid stench that hovered over the hill like a hungry mist ready to devour anything, or anyone, that entered its path. It was an unnatural odour, a malevolent stink. It was the stench of hatred. It had long been believed that it began with two local farmers, who's good relations were soiled by the matter of which one of them owned a particular area of farmland that nestled neatly between their homes on the slope of the giant hillside, and that this quarrel had passed, unresolved, through the generations like a disease, forever raging, both unchecked and untreated. In truth, no one could say with confidence how it had all started, or even when for that matter, for this dispute was almost as old as the hill itself and was, even at the time of this story, steeped more in legend and hearsay than any semblance of history. However, it is in the midst of this feud that our story begins.

It was the ninth year of the reign of King James, first here of that name, sixth in his parent land of Scotland; the Protestant son of a disgraced Catholic mother. England had survived the turmoil of the Tudor monarchy, enriched though it was by the grandeur and success of the last of them – Good Queen Bess as she was known-and was now seated firmly in position as a prominent world power. Life had never been as good-if you were lucky enough to be a person of wealth and standing that is. Unfortunately for most of those living in the wilds of the north, this grandeur and success was nought but a fairy tale, a distant dream that had absolutely no relevance to their poor and wretched existence. They were happy enough that was true, for they had never known any different, and had long since learnt to live with their situation, yet for these people their lives were just as hard as they had ever been; food was scarce, disease was not. There was little hope of improvement, little hope of anything except death. This was the reality for the young girl standing at the window of the draughty old farmhouse, pulling her willowy blonde hair back into a loose ponytail as she watched the small child collecting wood in the field behind. This was her life, it was her mother's life, it would be the child's life – and discounting the possibility of a miracle, or some other unlikely stroke of good fortune, it would continue in this way. Forever.

"Alison!" The voice from downstairs sharply penetrated

the silence.

"Are ye getting up or are we going to starve today?"

 "Aye I'm just coming Ma!" she shouted, pulling her cloak from the rear of the chair and starting for the door.

Sprinting down the stairway and into the kitchen she was momentarily stunned by the sight of the woman slumped in the old wooden chair beside the fire, her face turned inwards as though studying the flames. Silently she knelt before the chair and began to remove the tattered, hole-ridden shoes, taking care as not to disturb their owner, and placed them together on the stone floor. Alison looked at the sleeping figure, her face as worn and haggard as her footwear, her bony arms wrapped around her chest in an embrace against the cold. Smiling to herself, Alison wrapped an old blanket of wool around her grandmother's chest and gently pulled the chair nearer the warmth of the fire, for the old woman must not get too cold during these winter months. That done, she finally headed for the door.

And so Alison set off on another day's begging through the Lancashire countryside, with no certainty of gain, nor any consideration of risk or harm. For her, this was just another day; little did she know how the happenings of that early March morning would affect the lives of a number of people – of families- in the area as she held her hands out for anything that generosity afforded her on her travels. For Alison, her family, and the many other unsuspecting casualties of the events, today would mark the beginning – the beginning of the end.

2

Our story must then, undoubtedly, begin with the young lady with whom you have recently been acquainted.

As she pushed her way through the bitter winter winds into the dense wastelands in the shadow of the hill, the only thought present in Alison's mind was of the business of the day. She had to make enough money to feed the family that night else they would starve. She *had* to: her grandmother was far beyond the age in which she could be expected to provide, and the child was too young. Her mother could have engaged in a similar pursuit elsewhere, that was true, but she had not the benefit of youth and beauty with which to make advantage as did Alison, and was more than aware of it. James was of little use, his simplicity providing more of an obstacle than assistance that could be of benefit to his kin. No, the sustenance of the family lay in her small, white hands. That decided she hastened on in the early morning light, down Slipper Hill and over the ancient paths of the deserted northern fields.

She was quite out of breath by the time she reached

Colne Edge. Placing the battered straw basket on the summit of a wall, she paused to steady herself for a moment, her side aching from the speed of her stride.

"Good morning to ye" came a voice from the other side of the wall. Alison raised her head to look at her companion.

"To ye also" she responded, her lips curling into an amiable smile, for before her stood the face of one of her cousins. The young man returned the smile.

"Where ye off too at this young hour?" he continued, a note of inquisitiveness in his voice.

"Trawden way" Alison shrugged her shoulders lightly as though she herself was not entirely sure of her destination. "We need to eat".

He needed no more explanation and asked no further questions. Stooping his head slightly he silently bade her farewell and took his leave. Alison watched him as he walked away, his heavy boots crunching the stones beneath his feet, before once more taking up her basket and resuming her journey.

Down through North Valley she went, passing very few people for the hour was still early. Where she did encounter others, she held out her hands or the basket and begged aid of them. Some took pity and gave her items of food or the occasional dull coloured coin, but most simply walked on by, ignoring her pleas or pretending not to see the poor, dishevelled young girl before them. Alison quickly grew weary and longed to be at home before the fire. More than once she thought about turning around and heading back; only the image of her starving family made her press on with the enterprise. She could not let them down. The wind was beginning to fade, the day moving away from the early hours of dawn and into the more congenial sphere of the early morning. The sun, what little of it was ever seen in these parts, took its seat in the heavens and set about the awakening of the wild flowers that lined the paths on which she walked. Bluebells and daisies reached upwards towards the pale blue ceiling, their petals kissed by the occasional passing of a wandering bumblebee. Alison could not resist running her hand through their groups as she passed by, their heads soft beneath her fingers and damp with the remainder of the dew drops that had fallen in the previous hours. Occasionally she would come across one that had fallen foul of a now unseen creature, its beauty now adorning the floor rather than the stem on which it had once stood, and would place it carefully in her basket; it was of little use now, she reasoned and besides, her grandmother could use it to make the medicines that she was famous for. As her collection of flower heads increased in the basket Alison could not help wishing she could turn them into loaves of bread; by trading or by magic, she wasn't too bothered, after all a mound of pretty coloured petals would not go too far in feeding a family of five. For the moment, they were all she had.

Suddenly the sound of heavy footsteps could be heard in the distance. Alison's heart flapped within her chest, partly through the fear that she may come across a dangerous stranger while alone in such desolate surroundings, but also in anticipation that the approaching person may be one to look kindly on a tired, weary and destitute girl. The footsteps came steadily closer, eventually revealing a man travelling in her direction; his body slumped beneath the weight of the pack upon his back. He was a rough looking man, Alison noted, although it was hard to see whether his blackened, coarse face was due more to an arduous journey and workload than any indication of character. She could tell he was a peddler. Cautiously she continued forwards, her hand tightly gripping the handle of the basket. The wind, although much calmer now, was still playing in the fields, it's rapid movement making Alison acutely aware of the holes in her garments. Pulling her clothing as tightly around her body as she could with her free hand, she resolved to ask the foreigner for pins.

"Please sir" she stammered, holding the ripped materials out for him to see.

The man looked at her, his eyes betraying a sense of disgust at the sight of her. Without a word he made attempt to continue on his way, only to find the exhausted girl once more blocking his path.

"Please sir" she repeated, "I'm in need of pins, if you please. Look sir, I ask of you, look!" she once more flapped the garment out at the stony faced man.

"My dear" he started firmly, "It has been a long day, I am tired and all I want is to quench my thirst at the nearest ale-house"

"Some pins, sir, that's all I ask of you!"

"No, I have no pins I'm sure" came the reply, "and I have no will to remove this heavy bag from my back to look for them. Now please, allow me to pass".

Alison stood firm, more out of desperation than courage. A pair of rough hands grabbed at her upper arms, causing her to gasp in a combination of shock and fear. She felt herself being pushed backwards.

"I have no time for this" the man almost spat in her face, "I'm tired and hungry and do not wish to be bothered by a silly peasant girl like you! Now, kindly stand aside and let me go on my way!" he accentuated the finally statement with the sudden and unexpected release of her arms. She felt herself fall to the ground, her long hair tumbling over her face. Rubbing her arms, she watched the man walk briskly away from her, the tears welling up in her eyes. She had only wanted some pins.

"A curse be upon ye!" she shouted after him, her voice cracked with distress.

There was a strange sensation on her right arm. Lowering her head she noticed that she had a new companion; it was a dog. She had seen him before; he lived somewhere near her, although she had no idea whom he may have belonged to. He stood by her side, its head level with hers as she sat on the ground, its huge tongue running coarsely over the redness on her limbs. Wearily she rested her head against his thick black coat, the tears streaming down her dust stained cheeks.

"A curse be upon ye" she whispered again, her voice muffled by the dog's fur, "may God strike ye down where ye stand! A curse be upon ye!"

Abruptly the wind began to gather momentum once more, whipping through the fields with a haunted howling sound that shattered the silence. The world felt to be spinning around her. Alison snapped her eyes closed and shook her head but to no avail, the situation was no more improved when she opened them again a second or two later. The dog jumped to its feet, barked once into the air and bounded away into the distance, disappearing behind the trees almost as quickly as he had appeared moments earlier. There was a scuffling sound behind her, followed by a dull thud as something hit the ground. Alison turned to look in the direction of the noise. It was him; the peddler man. She climbed to her feet and ran to him as fast as she was able. He lay in the centre of the path; his body slumped into a heap, a low groaning coming from his lips. Laying a cold white hand upon his shaking forehead she tried to speak, but no words would come from her mouth as she looked upon the miserable wretch at her feet. He looked at her, a blank expression on his face. Alison didn't know what to do. The sound of voices could be heard, seemingly coming that way. She didn't know who they were, but was sure they would know how to help the poor peddler man who lay motionless where he had fallen. Quietly she clambered once more to her feet and wiped the tears from her eyes. There was nothing more she could do for him; she had to leave him in the care of the approaching group. Setting off at a brisk pace she made her way in her original direction. Barely a hundred yards away from the scene she came face to face with the oncoming couple – a man and woman in a cart pulled by a shabby chestnut horse whom she recognised as being folks from her side of the hill. Looking nervously over her shoulder at the injured man, she darted behind a nearby tree from where she could watch and make sure he was taken care of. Her heart rolled like a drum within her chest.

From her hiding place she heard a squeal as the pair came upon the obstacle in their path. She watched as first the woman, and then her husband climbed down from the cart to attend to the peddler man. Gripping the slimy damp trunk before her she strained to see what was happening as carefully the invalid was lifted from his position and placed onto the rear of the wooden cart. He didn't move once, not that she could see anyway. At length the cart and its three passengers rattled slowly on through the field, the creaking of its wheels still audible for a while after it could no longer be seen. Silence once more descended over the area. Alison waited for what seemed an eternity before creeping out from her concealment. She stood for a moment, the events of the previous few minutes whizzing through her head as she tried to understand what had just happened in that space before turning on her heels and running as fast as her aching legs would carry her towards home.

Her face was a strange colour of white by the time she reached the old farm building on the slope of Pendle Hill. Tearing past the half blind old woman still seated before the fire where Alison had left her some hours previously, she ran up the staircase and pushed the door firmly closed behind her, the tattered, dust ridden cloak discarded onto the bedroom floor like a piece of unwanted rubbish. The tears flowed freely now, their wetness pinning the straggled blonde hair to her colourless skin in a way not too dissimilar to the dog in the field. Deflated she threw herself down into the corner of the room; her knees pulled tightly into her chest and sobbed.

"This wasn't supposed to happen" she whispered into the darkness, her voice broken by heavy sobs. The face of the man kept flashing in her mind, his mouth dropped to one side, his eyes blank. It was all her fault. She had heard the whispers that had echoed around the hill for as long as she had been alive – probably even longer than that; she knew that her grandmother was regarded and feared as a dangerous witch, and her mother too. There was even talk of it being hereditary. She had never taken much notice of such things. And now this had happened. She couldn't get rid of the image; it was almost as though he were still there with her. She stared into the emptiness in shock; she had cursed a man and it had been fulfilled. Crouched in the corner of the draughty, bare room Alison wasn't too sure whether she wanted the power she was now convinced she held, the power of holding a person's fortune – nay his very life – within her hands was far too great a responsibility for her young mind to comprehend. No, she didn't want it at, not at all. But there was no doubt about it: the magic that had been talked about for many years was true – it existed! She was a witch; a *real* witch. She felt physically sick.

3

For hours she cowered in that corner, her eyes red with the weeping of a broken heart, her body convulsing with the fear and disbelief of that morning's happenings. Sitting in the absolute silence she heard the thumping of the old woman downstairs as she went about her daily business, the barking of hounds in the land beyond the half-open window, the banging of the wooden door as her sister ran in and out of the building, busily engaged in some childish activity. She heard the sound of her own thoughts echoing through her head until she could no longer stand to listen. Climbing to her feet, Alison knew what she had to do.

There was no way of telling how quickly she ran back through those fields that afternoon, except to say that her breath was short and raspy by the time she reached the edge of Colne market town and her entire body hurt with the exertion. She had no idea where she was going, much less of where the pair of kindly Samaritans had taken the injured man after driving him away in their cart. She didn't even know where to start looking. Dazed and anxious she made her way through the busy streets, for once oblivious to the disgusted expressions on the faces of those she passed on the way, her wide eyes searching for any small clue as to the man's whereabouts. Even the smell of the food on the many stalls went unnoticed, hungry though she was; so firmly fixed was her mind on the mission she had to undertake. She *had* to see him again. She considered asking a passer-by for information in the hope that someone would know what had happened to him; indeed she set her mind to it until she remembered that she didn't even know his name. It appeared to be an impossible task.

After what felt like hours of wandering listlessly through the streets Alison felt her legs growing weak beneath her. Finally she succumbed to their silent persuasion and sunk slowly onto the damp- cold stone doorstep of the nearest building, the sudden chill of it piercing her thin clothing, causing her exhausted skin to tingle at its touch. There she sat and watched the townsfolk going about their business; the grocer re-filling his vegetable baskets after the morning's sales, the baker in his crisp white apron bringing out his latest batch of offerings to tempt the passing crowds, the farmers keeping check on the livestock they had brought to market to sell on – for both breeding and slaughter; the people of Colne were earning their living. How she wished she were a part of that business; that she could head home that evening with pockets filled with the shiny coins that she had seen changing hands that day. There would be no more ribs protruding through sallow skin, or stomachs aching from the pull of hunger. No more begging for scraps of food from people who cared not whether you lived or died. No more stealing or fighting or...

Alison's dreamy thoughts of a life somewhat better than her own were sharply interrupted by the sound of voices not far from her resting place. They were women's voices, their shrillness tainted with the indisputable air of gossip. Usually Alison would have paid little heed to such chatter, for the lives of these far-removed people held no interest to her, except for one thing; the subject. She strained her ears to hear closer.

"Aye" she heard one dumpy looking woman declare, her heavy arms crossed firmly across her more than ample chest, "a peddler man they say"

"A terrible business" chirped another, "found in the old Colne field toward Trawden Forest. They reckon it was…" The woman checked quickly around her to see who may be listening. She didn't notice Alison in her doorstep hideout. Turning back to her group she lowered her voice to an almost whisper as she added "witchcraft".

Alison felt her stomach tighten into a knot as the gaggle of women each let out an audible gasp. Witchcraft was not something that respectable people talked about in the street, or at all if truth be told, and certainly not something one wanted to be thought of as being involved in. Magic was one of those things that everyone believed in, but nobody mentioned aloud; that all were interested in, in the way of morbid fascination, and at the same time all were terrified of. The King had outlawed it through all consuming fear. Witches were evil.

Alison knew little of this. Her simple life on the slopes of Pendle Hill was far enough removed from the realms of perceived civilisation that the declarations of the king and parliament rarely, if ever, reached their ears. She knew what magic was of course -folklore and legend had as big a place in poverty as it did in riches, and she had heard the rumours surrounding her own folk, but the hysteria surrounding such practices had, thus far, escaped her knowledge. The knot in her stomach and the sudden feeling of sickness that overcame her was due, in the main, to the knowledge that they were talking about what *she* had done, the man *she* had injured. Closing her eyes and breathing deeply she prepared to hear more.

"He's in a bad way, by all accounts" the fat woman continued. "Was happen a good job old Robinson and his wife were passing by that way and were like to find him, lying as he was, stricken in the grass or he might have met his end in that place."

The other women nodded, almost in time with each other as they listened.

"I hear the poor man is laid up in The Greyhound" she continued, revelling in her tale. "They say he might not live".

The church bells clanged loudly, breaking up the conversation as each of the three women bid their friends good day and went their separate ways. Moments later Alison stepped out from the doorway and ran, bitter tears streaming warmly down her cheeks, in the direction of The Greyhound Inn.

Her whole body shook as she looked at the alehouse in the centre of the main street. She desperately wanted to go in, to seek out the peddler man and see his condition for herself, to beg his forgiveness for her now bitterly regretted actions. How she wished she had never uttered that curse upon him. She hadn't known the consequences; had she done so she may well have thought twice. Alison's mother had always chided her for her rashness. She had always lost her temper with far too much ease, just as she had that day, and now she was being punished for it. Punished by a higher power than her mother – or so it seemed. She could taste the tears as they continued to fall, their salty flavour stinging on her tongue. People continued their day around her, edging, sometimes pushing rudely past her as she stood looking at the wooden Inn door. Her mind whirled with questions: should she go in and complete her mission? Should she turn and run home to her family? Why was this happening to her? Her head began to ache with the pressure. In time she summoned some strength from deep within herself and crept timidly toward the door. It opened with a loud squeak, helped on its way by a balding man in too-tight clothing. Alison shrunk into herself, her eyes cast downwards, for she was more than aware that she was well out of place there. She felt his glare pierce her skin like a poker and stepped apprehensively to one side to let him pass.

The inn was almost empty, save for a few men not unlike the one she had encountered in the doorway. Alison gazed around the wood panelled room, her eyes darting from left to right as though keeping watch for any creeping predators. And there he was; the peddler man.

He lay on one of the old wooden benches in the corner of the room; his long right leg draped carelessly off the edge and heaped lifelessly on the filthy floor. She couldn't see his face clearly but he appeared to be asleep. Cautiously she crept in his direction, her mind whirring with things to say to him should he be awakened, but in truth she knew not what would happen if the poor man set eyes on her again. He would blame her for his condition, that much she knew, and he would be right to do so. She blamed herself. Worse still, her appearance could send him into a fit of hysteria which would only serve to impede his recovery. She had already caused him so much pain; she would not be able to bear it if she was to be the cause of more suffering on his part. Quickly she turned on her heels and ran from the building, neither slowing nor stopping until she reached the top of the market street and the inn was out of her sight. Breathing deeply she turned and headed for home. He was breathing; that was all she needed to know. The peddler man was alive.

The sun was beginning to set by the time Alison reached the run down farmhouse that she called home. It was strangely quiet, almost as though something was waiting on the other side of the wooden door; something not altogether pleasant. Gently she pushed the door and tiptoed inside, pulling the ribbons of her cloak to release its embrace of her and hanging it on the makeshift hook on the wall before turning to meet the steely glare of her mother not five steps away from where she stood.

"Where the devil have ye been till this time young lady?" Alison studied the hay strewn floor, not daring to lift her eyes even for a second. The thin, foreboding looking woman repeated her question

"Well?...... are ye gonna give an account of thyself missy?. I asked ye, where *have* ye been?"

Alison opened her mouth to answer, but no sound emerged. Her throat was dry and sore and she was unable to form the needed words. She sniffed once and lowered her head still further. Her mother took a step towards her.

"I asked ye a question!" the shrill voice increased its

volume, "and where is the

basket....have ye brought *nothing* for us to eat?"

Alison shuffled on the spot, well aware that the basket lay on the floor of the room above their heads, and did not – as correctly predicted by her mother- contain anything in the way of food. Her head began to spin. Swiftly she ran past the cross-armed mother, her eyes still firmly fixed downwards, and sprinted up the rickety staircase towards her bedroom sanctuary. She could hear the voice float up behind her as she half slammed the door behind her.

"Oh, so we all gonna starve today then?"

Alison covered her ears with her hands in a vain effort to shut out the words. Through her thin, bony fingers she heard the words,

"Well, curse ye then ye miserable wretch!"

Curled up behind the door, Alison felt her mother's curse was a little too late.

4

And what of the peddler man?

The kindly pair of strangers in the fields had loaded his ailing body onto their cart and carried him the short distance to the aforementioned Greyhound Inn on Colne's market street. There they had left him in the care of the Innkeeper and his wife; a benevolent couple who gave him as much attention as they were able to spare. His rescuers looked in on him daily and made generous contributions to his upkeep, which his hosts appreciated for they were not the most affluent of people themselves despite their business. The innkeepers made him comfortable. He was provided with a warm room and a comfortable bed, although he was not in it at the time of Alison's first visit as it was not, as yet ready for occupation. By nightfall he was tucked up in almost white bed sheets and left to drift into much needed slumber.

Before then though, the innkeepers had discovered – through his personal items, for he was unable to tell them himself – that his name was Lawe, John Lawe, and that his main address was in the town of Halifax, which lay over the border in the county of Yorkshire. With his signalled permission, Mr Innkeeper had penned a letter in which he explained his patient's condition and his current whereabouts, and addressed the envelope to one Mr Abraham Lawe. The note was dispatched at speed and the Mr returned to his work.

Abraham Lawe arrived three days later.

He was a tall man, with broad shoulders and a square jaw. He strolled into the Greyhound Inn and introduced himself, asking politely if he may be allowed to see his sick father. The little innkeeper retold the story of the incident in Colne Field as they climbed the creaky staircase before ushering his guest into the required room. Bowing politely he took his leave and let them be.

The room was in semi darkness, the thin material at the windows still closed from the recently departed night. Abraham pulled them sideways to let in the dismal daylight and turned to see his father for the first time. He gasped as he did so, for the sight before him was, at best, pitiful. The older man lay motionless in the bed, the left side of his mouth drooped downwards, the residue of saliva running from the gape left behind. His arms were placed by his sides, above the turned down bedclothes. Abraham's eyes filled with tears at the plight of his father. Pulling up a chair, he sat by the bed and took him by the hand. It was clear that the gesture could not be reciprocated; the patient strained to do so but was unable.

John Lawe was paralysed.

So Abraham sat with his father and wept silently for his condition. John was glad of his company and despaired at his own incapacity. Together they wiled away the long hours until the darkness set in, wherein the son kissed his father tenderly on the forehead and bid him goodnight.

In his own room, Abraham passed an uncomfortable night. Tossing and turning continuously, the image of the sick man in the room across the landing playing repeatedly in his mind. If he did happen to drift off to sleep, the pictures invaded his dreams causing him to cry out in horror and awaken in a state of anxiety. In the end he lay on the bed and wondered what he might do to help his father or, how he may be able to avenge his misfortune. The innkeeper had told him that there had been an argument with a local girl immediately before his being taken ill, but had he told him who she was? Abraham couldn't remember. That is what he needed; the name of the girl with his father when he collapsed. He needed to know what had happened and only she could tell him. He resolved to discover her identity, along with those of the rescuers. He would start in the morning.

Dawn arrived with a dull light and a slate coloured sky. Abraham crawled out from beneath the blankets and pulled aside the thin grey material that barely covered the windows. The day had already started beneath him; the shopkeepers had thrown open their doors, the stallholders had arranged their wares and the townsfolk were about their business. He stood and watched them, wondering with each new body whether the girl was among them. Was she the young girl with the milk churns across the street? Was the baker's daughter the one who had harmed his father? He searched the scene from above, finding no answer to the question, the imagined face of his prey whirling round in his mind. Finally he dragged himself away from the window, pulled on his clothes and left the room.

John Lawe looked comfortable as his son poked his head around the door. Not wishing to disturb the much needed rest, the younger man decided to leave him be for a while. He pulled the door closed, making every effort to abort the thunderous creak of its movement, and made his way downstairs. The innkeeper's wife was about the business of cleaning the bar, her flabby white arms thrusting back and forth in such vigour that he believed she may make a hole in the top of the woodwork with the ragged wash cloth. She raised her head to look at him as he approached, a chestnut brown curl hanging loosely over her forehead having foraged an escape from beneath her cream-white cap.

"Mornin" she beamed, "ye manage to sleep well?"

Abraham nodded in acknowledgement of the question

and sat himself down on the stool.

"Ale?"

"Aye, why not?" he answered.

"Why not indeed!" she winked, pouring him a beaker and setting it down before him, "there ye go – on th' house!"

Abraham thanked her and took the glass. The ale was cold, hitting the back of his throat like a wave on a beach. He was more than glad of it.

"How's ye father this morning?" the woman asked. Abraham looked into her oval shaped face and saw her genuine concern.

"Pretty much the same" he replied, "he seems comfortable enough, I'm pleased for that!"

She placed a chubby hand onto his arm.

"I'm glad for that too" she said, "he gave us all such a scare when he arrived, as though the devil himself was in him".

Abraham flinched, the reference sounding more than ominous in his mind. He pushed his elbow further onto the bar top and leaned towards her conspiratorially.

"What do ye know, about what happened to him?" he whispered.

The woman mirrored his position on the opposite side of

the bar.

"I believe…" she began, "that there may have been an altercation with a Pendle girl".

"Go on" Abraham urged her.

"It was Old Farmer Robinson and his wife who brought him here. Said they'd found him stricken in the grass in Colne Field, much as you saw him yesterday".

"And the girl?" Abraham inquired.

"Hmm her" came the response. She saw the puzzled, anxious look on the face of her guest and her heart twitched within her chest.

"Look deary" she continued, "I aint one to gossip, and there's no actual proof she was involved in owt…."

"But she was there – when he fell ill?" Abraham was becoming desperate

"Well…yes…so it is believed" she conceded. "Old Robinson's wife said she saw her in the trees as they passed through the scene. But still……."

"Then she must be found" he cut in, unable to pay heed to any more excuses on this girl's behalf. "She could hold the answers".

The woman bowed her head and studied her hands for a moment, unsure as to what to say next.

"Do you know her?" he continued, sensing her discomfort.

"I know *of* her" she answered, with a small shrug of her shoulders. "I've seen her around once or twice but I can't say as I know her".

"Look dear. There's two sorts of folks round here; those that's respectable, and those that ain't. You don't wanna go messing with folks such as her".

Abraham's eyes widened. He was intrigued.

"Folks such as her" he repeated, "however do you mean?"

The woman dashed the cloth down onto the surface of the bar and leaned forward.

"Like I said, I'm not one to gossip, and there may be no good reason for the talk that you hear around here….."

"…..but……." her listener interjected.

"They say her grandmother is a witch, a dark witch: her mother too. They reckon

Old Demdike – the older woman – bewitched one of Nutter's cows over at Bullhole Farm, and that she was able to turn milk into butter by using a charm.

There's talk of murder too – death by magic as it were. It runs in the family – it's like bad blood."

There was a moments silence as Abraham tried to understand what she was saying.

"As I said" the woman continued. "There's those that it's best to stay clear of. The likes of Alison Device and her family are the kind of family a good man doesn't wish to interfere with".

"Just my advice" she shrugged, leaving him to his own thoughts.

And what thoughts they were. Death by magic, witch, murder; the words echoed through his head. Had this girl tried to kill his father? Was magic the cause of the horrific vision in the bedroom upstairs? Surely so, for he had paid a visit to his father before he left Halifax the evening before the incident; he had been fine and well then, and in quite high spirits. What ailment could have possibly afflicted him between then and his reaching the field, and the girl at the centre of it all? None as far as Abraham could work out. And now he knew of her name; what had the innkeeper's wife called her – Alison Device, that was it. He knew who she was and now, by the strength of God he would find her.

But how? He now knew who she was, but not where she might be found and, being a stranger in these parts, he had little chance of tracking her down by himself. He needed help, or at the least, information. Finishing his ale in one mouthful he placed the beaker down and climbed off the stool.

Outside the rain was just beginning to fall. It pelted the tops of the market stalls and roofs of the buildings that lined the dismal grey streets like a constant rhythmic drum beat. Puddles gathered at every available stopping place like the huddles of gossips who watched the day go by, their business running through the town like a continuous, never ending tide. Abraham pulled up the collar of his coat and hurried down the street.

5

For a whole week Abraham Lawe wandered the streets of Pendle. Each morning, after looking in on his father and attending to any little need he may have, he would set out from The Greyhound Inn and seek out anybody who may have the information he required for his mission. He asked about this Alison Device girl to any person he met upon the way, but with little success, for no one wished to either involve themselves or admit that they might now where she could be found. Every question was answered with a shrug of the shoulders or a shocked expression, followed quickly by a swift dismissal of the subject. It appeared that when she had said that this girl was one to be avoided, the innkeeper's wife may have been right.

On the eighth day of his search, Abraham rose as usual, paid his morning visit to the room across the hall where the older man lay in recovery, and took his leave of the inn once more. He was becoming weary of wandering, almost aimlessly around the area, meeting the same people again and again and receiving the same answers to his queries. His feet ached at the end of every day, and his heart too with the disappointment of not being able to help his father by finding his assailant. He was beginning to consider giving up the search.

Slowly he trudged up the Market street in Colne for what felt like the hundredth time, his shirt damp and clinging to his back under the heat of the midday sun, his only thought consisting of getting himself indoors and a cool drink down his aching throat. He didn't notice the small group of women as he stomped past them, that is to say he didn't *take* notice of them for he had to swerve from his path in order to avoid them. He of course realised they were there, but so transfixed on his destination was his mind at that point that they were an irrelevance. Until he heard one of them speak.

"I told ye" one deep female voice uttered sternly, "that Device girl is from bad stock. Why, only one of *their* kind would be so bold as to come to market as though nowt had happened. No shame that lot, I tell ye!"

Abraham stopped dead in his tracks at the mention of that name; the name that was etched in his memory like a carving – Alison Device.

For a week everyone had denied knowledge of her and her whereabouts, and now these women may have the answers he was looking for. He turned quickly and addressed the group.

"I'm sorry ladies" he began as they face him questioningly, "I couldn't help but hear what ye were saying just then. Were you referring to young Alison

Device?"

"Aye" answered the deep voiced woman sharply

"What of it?"

Suddenly Abraham realised. These people did not know who he was, although it was clear they knew of the incident with his father. He bowed slightly and introduced himself.

"My name is Lawe, Abraham Lawe. It was my father who was found in the field the other week, after some kind of meeting with this Device child"

The women gasped in unison at his words.

Abraham continued.

"I have spent these last few days looking for the girl. Nobody will give me any information."

There was a small pause.

"I believe you have seen her recently?"

The woman who had spoken placed a hand on his arm. Abraham looked down at it and bowed his head again.

"Mighty sorry about your favver" she said, "must have been a shock to ye. Twas a shock to all er us"

Abraham nodded in response, hoping that that was not the end of the conversation.

"It's no surprise though, that folk don't wanna talk about it" she continued. Abraham said nothing; it seemed perfectly clear that people *did* want to talk about it, and that that was all that was being talked about at the minute. It wasn't *it* they didn't want to talk about, it was *her.* He stood and allowed the woman to speak more.

"We is simple folks around here; simple folks with simple lives. We don't want no hassles from the likes of such as them that live on the hill. Its not that they're poor folk – we're none of us all that well off round 'ere – it's that they're *unpleasant* folk, if ye take heed of the talk around 'ere that is".

Abraham knew exactly what she meant, the talk of witchcraft and magic was rife about the whole area.

"But you've seen her?" he pressed on, eager for the information.

"Aye, she was 'ere, this morning, in the market.

Begging for scraps like a dog, bold as ye like!

She's gone now though, headed off up yonder not too long since." She pointed over her shoulder towards the top of the road. "Heading back home I shouldn't wonder".

Abraham inhaled sharply at the news. Thanking them heartily and shaking each of them by the hand he bade them farewell and set off up the street. The end was almost within his grasp. He could almost smell his prey.

On reaching the summit of the street, Abraham Lawe took a right turn and headed over Colne Edge. The ancient hill stood before him, its crown hidden behind a large mist that sat ominously over its head. The hill itself was a dark colour of green, so dark in fact that it was almost a scorched brown. There was nothing to be seen upon its sides besides the occasional building, placed seemingly miles away from any of its neighbours, and splatterings of trees and bushes that decorated its slopes. To Abraham Lawe it looked like nothing but bleak, barren land.

He stomped on through the long grass, the cracking of the occasional branch beneath his feet the only sound to be heard. Something moved in the bushes ahead of him; the rustling sound almost deafening in the thunderous silence. Abraham peered into the undergrowth, screwing his eyes up tightly to get a clearer view; he could see something within the greenery, something white. He needed to get closer. Carefully he crept forwards and stooped, his hatless head almost resting against the branches as he stared through a gap in its body. Suddenly he pulled away, his eyes widened at the sight before him. It was an eye; and it was looking straight at him. A few seconds later, after recovering his composure, he looked again. There was nothing to be seen except for the inside of the hedgerow and the grass that sat on the other side. He straightened his aching body back into a standing position, told himself that he had imagined it, and prepared to continue his journey. That was until he noticed the face.

It was the white, almost ghost like face of a young girl, her wide dull grey eyes staring at him from the top of the bushes in such a way that a shiver ran coldly down the centre of his spine; indeed Abraham felt that, rather than looking *at* him, she was looking *through* him. She was not particularly pretty, although he had seen many less attractive girls than this one, but there was something strangely captivating about this chalk – white vision that stood in the middle of the field in the shadow of Pendle Hill. Her long blonde hair hung around her head, its curls cemented by an invisible layer of grease that made them shine unnaturally in the sunlight against her waxen skin, mottled with the markings of some bygone illness alongside the bad skin of an adolescent. Abraham inhaled sharply and took a step backwards in astonishment. The girl however, didn't move.

"I'm s..s..sorry!" he stammered, almost as though he were out of breath.

"I didn't see you there".

There was no reaction, save for a slight flicker of her eyelids.

"Are you okay?" he asked, stepping once more towards

the hedge. Still she said nothing. Abraham studied her for a moment, unsure of his next move. The silence was becoming uncomfortable. He shuffled his feet and tried to divert his gaze from hers, but with little success. He couldn't take his eyes from her. A dog barked in the distance. Abraham awoke from his trance with a jolt as the girl whirled her head around to locate the source of the noise. Out of the trees bounded a dog, a dog the size of a bear cub, with long black fur and eyes of a dull red colour. It ran towards the girl and rolled at her feet; she laughed as she watched it and lowered herself at the knees to rub its smooth underbelly. Abraham smiled to himself at the sight, for this was the first movement she had made since her sudden appearance those ten or so minutes earlier. Now, as she played tenderly with the mass of black on the ground, she was beginning to seem more lifelike, more human.

He stood there for a good few minutes before she remembered he was there, reminded no doubt by the crunch of a branch beneath his boots as he shuffled his feet. Swiftly she raised her head and flashed him a yellow toothed smile as she pulled herself to her feet.

"I know you don't I?" she half whispered.

Abraham looked confused.

"I seen you, in th' market over Colne. You're with the peddler man ain't ye?"

This time it was Abraham's turn to be silent.

"Is he ye favver?" she continued. Abraham managed a slight nod of acknowledgement. The girl lowered her eyes as the dog yelped and retreated playfully back in the direction of the trees.

"Is he well?" she continued "I mean, is he getting better? I didn't mean it when I cursed him. I didn't think owt'd come of it. I never meant for that to happen – honest I didn't. If I'd have known…."

Abraham's head began to whirl. She was speaking so quickly, her words ran off her tongue almost incomprehensibly; he had to strain to understand her. But he *did* understand. "Are you…" he began, his voice shaking

"Are you Alison Device?"

The girl lowered her head and closed her eyes as she wished with every bone in her body that that was not her name. But it was, and there was little use denying it.

"Aye" she whispered. "That be my name".

"Then you must come with me now" Abraham said decisively, "Come with me and see how he is for yourself".

Alison stepped back in surprise. She had already seen him, the day she had visited him at The Dog,, the day it had all happened; what use would it be to see him again?

"I'm sure he would like to see you" Abraham continued, eager to persuade her.

"Well…." She began, "I should like to say sorry I suppose"

"Good," came his brusque reply "then we shall go!".

There was little Alison could do but acquiesce to his request. Together they walked back towards Colne Edge; the tall broad shouldered man and the tiny stick like girl, with hardly a word spoken between them for the duration of their journey. In the field the black dog sat and watched them go before turning on its heels and galloping off into the distance.

6

In The Dog Inn, John Lawe was recovering comfortably; he was able to sit up better now, had regained most of his speech and was eating solid food once more. This was the condition in which the returning Abraham and his companion found him.

"Pa" Abraham cooed round the wooden door of the bar room, "I've brought someone to see you!" The older man beckoned him forward, wondering who his visitor could be. Abraham stepped into the room, with Alison hiding nervously at his rear. John strained to see her.

"Well" he irked, "who is it?"

Abraham stepped nonchalantly to the side and allowed his father to see his guest. John shrank back into his seat, his face a funny shade of white. He was more than aware of who this young girl was.

"Y…y…..you!" he stammered, the fear clearly audible in his voice.

"You….you did this….to me; in the field. You put a curse on me, and look. Look what you have done!"

Alison said nothing and stared earnestly at the floor. While the peddler man looked a great deal better than he had the last time she had seen him, she still could not quite bring herself to look him in the face; not properly at any rate. She was also painfully aware of the presence of others in the room, for the Inn was filling up with locals finishing work for the day. Her face felt like it was on fire as she stared endlessly at the wooden floorboards. Abraham saw her discomfort and it pleased him.

"Do you believe in magic miss?" John continued. Alison raised her eyes slightly before immediately dropping them again.

"Yes, sir" she muttered, hardly daring to speak the words aloud.

"I didn't catch that" her inquisitor retorted,

"I asked whether you believe in magic."

Alison reaffirmed her answer. She could feel the silence in the room as she spoke the words.

"Did you, or did you not, make a curse upon me, that day in the field?"

Alison nodded her head again, silently wishing she was anywhere but where she now stood.

"Do you hear that people?" Abraham shouted through the eerie quiet, "this child admits to using magic to lame this poor man; my father. She admits it here and now, and you all bear witness to her confession".

A low murmur rippled round the room. Abraham stood back and enjoyed the scene that was playing out before him.

"Well, miss" John said calmly, "what have you to say for yourself?"

Alison ran to the side of the chair and fell onto her knees.

"I'm sorry" she sobbed, warm salted tears running down her cheeks. "I'm so very sorry sir. I din't mean it, I just get cross sometimes and the words just come outta me mouth sir. I never meant ye harm, of course I didn't; I never harmed no one in me life sir. I wish this had never come about sir, truly I do. If only I could take it back. I'm so very sorry."

The words tumbled from her lips at speed, just as they had done earlier when she had met Abraham not two hours earlier. The eyes of the onlookers burned into her back as she wept quietly into her hands; she knew what they were thinking – these were the same people who had talked of the dark ways of her family for as long as she could remember, that had called her folks by the name of witch across the whole of the county. She knew they would now feel justified.

Something touched the top of her head. Alison looked up to see the hand of her accuser sliding away from her. She wiped her tears with the back of her hand and pushed her hair away from her face, where it had fallen when she had dropped to the floor. John looked at the wretched, dishevelled child that stood before him and his heart panged with concern. She looked so tiny as she knelt there, and so thin – indeed he well believed she hadn't eaten a full meal in quite some time. Could this poor thing really be as evil as to lame him by a curse? He had been so sure before, but now he just could not see it being true. At least she surely would not do such a thing *intentionally*, he thought. He had reached out to her to silence her weeping rambling – now he found himself speaking words he didn't think he would ever hear himself say, not even ten minutes ago:

"I forgive you!"

Alison stared at him through her tear stained eyes. These were not words she heard too often; indeed she couldn't recall ever hearing them before in her life. She wasn't too sure she actually understood his meaning. Seeing her confusion John laid his bony hand on her lower arm and repeated the words

"I forgive you!"

"But…but…but sir" Alison managed to stammer in astonishment, her heart quickening within her chest.

"But you're hurt, and it's all my doing!" the tears began to fall once more a she spoke the words.

"Nay missy" John whispered, "don't upset yourself. You came here and confessed your sins afore all these folks –

that's some courage indeed. I bear no ill will t'ward you, for you are just a child and know not what you do. Rest easy my dear. You are indeed forgiven".

"Th..th…th….thank you sir!" Alison could hardly believe what she was hearing. John nodded slowly and beckoned towards the door. For all her simplicity, Alison knew it was a sign of dismissal. Relieved, she curtseyed and headed for the door.

No one was more surprised about what had just happened than Abraham Lawe. He had spent the previous few days traipsing across the area hunting this girl down; he had found her and brought her to face her victim – his father – and for what? She had lamed him in malice and he wanted her to pay. Forgiveness! Abraham didn't think so. Helping his father back to his bedroom on the first floor he decided that the old man may have been deceived by the snivelling wretch that had thrown herself at his feet, but he hadn't. Silently Abraham resolved that this was not the end of the matter. He would think upon his next move.

7

Just over twelve miles away from The Dog Inn, Roger Nowell was sitting at his dining table enjoying his usual midday meal when there was a loud knocking at his door. Not wanting to be disturbed, he signalled to his manservant to answer the call and continued, only to find himself bothered minutes later by a request for an audience. Annoyed, he threw down his napkin and left the room.

In the entrance hall stood the figure of Abraham Lawe – tall, domineering and not altogether happy, his moody appearance not helped by the fact that he had slept little the previous night thanks to the confrontation at the Inn in Colne. He extended a rough hand to the gentleman and lowered his head slightly in respect. Nowell reciprocated the gesture.

"Abraham Lawe, sir" Abraham introduced himself. "I have a matter of some importance that I feel I must bring to your attention".

Roger was intrigued.

"Please Mr Lawe, come take a seat" he said, ushering his guest into the adjoining room and leading him to a chair. Abraham sat down.

"Now sir" he continued, "what is your business?"

Abraham swallowed hard, well aware that the story he was about to relate might sound almost unbelievable to some, particularly educated folk such as this Mr Nowell. But he had come this far, and this needed to be done. There was no turning back.

"I asked many folks who I should come to about this and I was given your name many times" he started. Roger nodded in encouragement.

"It's my father you see. He had a bit of a…how shall I say this…an incident a week or so ago. He was lamed by a local girl, by magic it would seem; in broad daylight."

Roger Nowell stroked his greying beard, his dull eyes lighting up at the sound of the word 'magic'. He had been waiting for this moment.

"Magic you say"

"Aye sir" said Abraham "they say she's a witch, from a family of witches. She admitted what she had done, in public sir"

Roger Nowell liked what he was hearing. He had a strange feeling that he already knew the family to whom his visitor was referring, or could at least narrow it down to a couple of local families. To be sure, he asked the question anyway.

"And the girl? You say she has confessed to witchcraft? You have witnesses I assume?"

"Aye sir, an inn full of them" came the reply.

"Who is the girl Mr Lawe?"

Again, Abraham swallowed hard before blurting out the words "The call her Alison Device".

Roger allowed himself a self contented smile. He was familiar with this family; he too had heard the whispers of dark magic around Pendle Hill, but had no evidence of its existence.

Now he may just have been given what he had been looking for.

Abraham continued to furnish the older gentleman with the details of the incident in Colne Field some twelve days or so earlier. Not wishing to trivialise the matter in hand, he even went so far as to relate as fact the mutterings of people on the street including the story of the huge black dog that was said to have attacked the peddler on Alison's orders and caused his infirmity. He reported the words of the curse more than once, telling Nowell that his father remembered them vividly as they were so heinous and powerful that they would never be forgotten; how she asked the powers of hell to strike her victim down dead for his refusal to help her by providing her with what she needed. Nowell listened intently, his lust for action growing with every revelation. Abraham was well aware that his story was, in part, a fabrication – or at least an embellishment of the truth, but he was so disgusted with his father's too easy forgiveness of his assailant that his desire for justice had reached far beyond the point of conscience. He wanted justice – or vengeance – and he wanted it quickly.

Nowell allowed him to tell the story without interruption, frantically scribbling on a notepad that had been sitting on the cabinet beside his chair anything and everything he deemed to be essential information. Abraham was glad of this, for he now believed that somebody was taking the matter seriously at last.

"Well Mr Lawe" Nowell stood up and extended his hand, which Abraham accepted readily.

"I find your story both fascinating and disturbing in equal measures. Thank you for bringing it to my attention. I shall make further enquiries and see what can be done"

"I thank you sir" replied Abraham courteously

"I appreciate you giving me your time".

And with that he left.

Roger Nowell returned to his lunch, his mind racing with the thought of witchcraft existing on his territory. This was just what he needed; the king would look favourably upon him should he succeed in ridding the world of such evil beings – his fear of magic being absolute – and may even lead to some kind of promotion or royal acknowledgement. Besides, it may provide a way of removing the attention away from his son's recent misdemeanours which were causing him no end of grief and misery. A successful prosecution for witchcraft would provide the perfect distraction. He immediately dispatched his servants and the horse and cart to bring the accused to him.

8

And so it was that Alison Device, her mother Elizabeth, and brother James arrived at Ashlar House to face the High Sheriff of Lancashire in the shape of Roger Nowell. They hadn't been told why they were summoned, or whom they were to see when they got there, but they knew one thing; important men like Nowell did not demand to see people like them for no reason.

They stood in the entrance hall, three dishevelled, undernourished people, and gazed around them in awe at the luxury which they had no idea existed. It was a far cry from the wild slopes of Pendle Hill.

At length they were directed into the same room that Abraham Lawe had stood in not two hours earlier. Nowell sat this time behind his desk, notepad open and pen in hand, his spectacles pinned firmly halfway down his nose. He rose as they entered and bowed his head.

"Ah" he began, partly taken aback at the appearance of his visitors.

"Alison Device I assume" he addressed Alison directly for she was, in truth, the only one whose name he actually knew.

"Aye sir" she replied with a slight curtsey.

"And this must be your mother and brother" he continued, gesturing to them in turn.

"Aye sir"

Nowell picked up a small silver bell that sat on his desk and shook it. The noise echoed around the mansion for what seemed like an eternity. The door opened and a man entered the room.

"Ah" Nowell said as he turned to address the newcomer. "I need to speak to these people individually. Could you see Mr and Mrs Device into the hallway and make them comfortable while I speak with the young lady?" with the last words he turned and smiled strangely at Alison. The man, whom Alison assumed was a servant of Newell's, whisked the mother and brother from the room and closed the door firmly behind them.

Alison stood before the desk, her slight frame shaking with fear; fear that she had been separated from her mother and had to speak with this man alone, fear that she had no idea as to why she should be there in the first place. Nowell resumed his seat behind the desk and looked her up and down, trying to catch any markings of evil that may be present upon her body. He could find none, at least none that stood out on that preliminary, long distance examination. He could tell that she was uncomfortable, which suited his purpose entirely. If this child was a witch, she was about to be discovered.

"Now child" he began, looking Alison directly in the face. "I hear you've had a spot of trouble of late".

Alison looked confused.

"I hear there was an incident not too long past, in Colne Field, with a Mr….."

He looked down at his notepad as though checking the name. In reality he knew full well what the name was, for he had been savouring the details for the hours between Abraham's visit and the one that was now taking place, but he didn't wish for her to know that.

"Mr….John Lawe" he continued, removing his spectacles from his face in one swift movement of his right hand. Alison was in no doubt as to what he was referring. Her whole body began to shake once more with panic. She had confessed to the peddler man the day before and he had been kind enough to forgive her; what did this man want with her? She stared at the floor, her top teeth chewing at her bottom lip in a motion not unlike like that of a rabbit, and tried her hardest to prevent herself from bursting into tears.

"I would like to hear what happened" he continued, "your side of the story, as it were".

Alison said nothing.

"May I ask you some questions, if you don't wish to tell me all in one go?" he offered, a note of kindness almost evident in his voice.

Alison nodded. That sounded like a better option to her, for she was not confident with words, nor with interviews with strangers. Nowell accepted this.

"Do you know who I am?"

Alison had never seen this man before in her life; gentlemen like him did not associate with folks such as her, the poor folk who did little more than plague their lives with their frequent begging and stealing. This man looked important, she thought to herself, but how should she know whom he was? She confirmed that she did not.

"Then I shall go no further until I have introduced myself. My name is Roger Nowell, magistrate of this borough and High Sheriff of Lancashire".

Alison did not quite understand the words, but even in her uneducated simplicity she could tell that she was in the presence of authority. She swallowed hard and cast a fleeting glance in his direction; he was looking at her above the rim of his spectacles, his eyes piercing her like a red hot poker. She averted her gaze at speed.

"Now then, to the matter in hand. Did you come across a Mr John Lawe in Colne on March 16th of this year?"

Alison nodded.

"And what, may I ask, was your business there on that

morning?"

"Begging sir"

"Begging?"

"Yes sir. We are poor folks and often have no food to eat. We have to beg to live sir. It's the only way".

"I see" Roger Nowell stroked his beard. "Go on".

"I only wanted some pins" she muttered.

"Pins?" Nowell inquired. He knew nothing of any pins. Abraham had not mentioned pins.

"Aye sir. My gown was torn and I needed pins with which to fix it. I asked the peddler man for some, but he was mean and said cruel things, and pushed me to the ground. I hurt me ankle sir, it really hurt and I cried sir. I said something in haste, something I wish I hadn't said, but I was angry sir, and hurt sir and…."
She could feel the tears forming in her eyes as she rushed the words out. Nowell looked at the pitiful child that stood before him and a lump formed in his throat. Summoning the manservant with a sharp ring of his bell, he demanded that she be brought water. The suited gentleman silently obeyed, returning moments later with a silver cup and handing it to Alison, who received it gratefully and took a large mouthful. Wet, cold and refreshing, she felt it slide down the back of her throat and was glad of it.

"Do you feel you can go on?" Nowell asked at length. Alison simply raised her eyes. Her inquisitor took it as confirmation that she was able to continue.

"You say Mr Lawe hurt you. Can you tell me more about that?"

"Aye sir. He was in a hurry to go on his way. He grabbed me by Th' arms and pushed me to Th' ground. Hurt me arms he did, they were red marked an' all."

"Quite. You mentioned that you may have said something that you maybe shouldn't have said.

Would you like to tell me what that was?"

"I did what I always do sir, when I get meself into madness. I cursed him sir, asked God to strike him down where he stood. It's what I've always done sir, as have my kin. They is just words sir, never meant no 'arm by it, not really sir. Words don't really hurt people, do they sir?"

"It appears that they do my dear, at least they have in this case"

Alison felt the familiar prick of tears once more. She hadn't meant to cause the peddler any actual harm, indeed she couldn't quite bring herself to believe that her words had been fulfilled – and so quickly. How she regretted her hasty utterings of that morning in the fields.

"I need to ask you one more question, if that's ok?" Nowell pressed, smelling his prey. He didn't even wait for an answer.

"Do you believe that what happened to Mr Lawe was done by your hand, by your words, by your use of evil powers?"

"Aye sir" came the reply; the reply he wanted so badly to hear. "I think it must 'ave been".

"And how long have you had such powers?"

"They say me folks have always had 'em sir. They say it's in the blood. I ne'er felt like a witch sir, not until the dog at the Rough Lee – the one that spoke to me as I walked on past it"
Nowell's eyes widened in anticipation. He was going to earn some great reward with this, he could feel it.

"A speaking dog you say?" he probed

"Aye sir, it asked me if I wanted special powers like my kinsfolk. Said I could have them freely in 'change for me soul. Do ye know what I mean sir?"

"I do indeed know what you mean. Now tell me, do you know of an Anne Whittle?"

"Old Chattox?" Alison almost snarled as she spoke the words. "That old witch?"

Nowell raised his eyebrows, causing his young

interviewee to inhale with an audible gasp as she realised what she had just said. But then, why shouldn't she say it she thought to herself. It would serve as revenge for what Chattox had said against her folks, accusing them of all kinds of evil doings –most of which she was more than likely doing herself – and besides, the most harm it that could come from this would be a slap on the wrist at worst. She, Alison Device, had already been labelled as a witch – as had her family – she was going to make sure that Anne Whittle was labelled too.

"Well she is" she added defiantly. "She killed me favver".

That was precisely the sort of thing Nowell wanted to hear. John Device's death almost eleven years earlier had officially been declared as being natural; there had never been any talk of there being anything suspicious about it. Anne Whittle – Old Chattox – had killed him? The only possible way would be by dark magic.

It wasn't enough. He needed more.

"Why would she kill your father?" he asked, urging her to continue. Alison was only too ready to go on.

"He owed her sir, or so she reckons. He paid her each harvest – nothing much, just a bit of meal, I can't remember what fer tho. Anyways, he didn't pay her and she got mad sir. Cursed him she did, and he died he did"

"Anything else?"

"Aye sir" Alison replied eagerly "in the same way she did to death Anne Nutter, and John Moore's daughter and Hugh Moore to tell of just three, and probley even more besides; evil she is sir!" Nowell looked at her over the rim of his spectacles.

"Well Miss Device, I think that is enough questions for today. Thank you for talking to me and I shall see you soon".

"Can I go now sir" Alison looked surprised, suddenly remembering her manners and adding a quick "please" to her request.

"Yes, yes" Nowell answered with a dismissive wave of his hand. Alison dipped in an awkward curtsey and sped towards the door. Once outside in the cool hallway she breathed deeply and collapsed in a heap on the floor.

Nowell, however, was ready for his next victim.

The moment Alison had left the room he had seated himself down at his desk and written down everything she had said in his notepad, a sly smile spreading across his face. She had been very helpful, he thought to himself, now it was time to see what the others were going to tell him.

9

Shortly after Alison's dismissal from the room, her mother was sent to face the questions of Roger Nowell. Standing before the great oak desk, and the well dressed gentleman to whom it belonged, Elizabeth Device could not help but wonder as to why she and her eldest children had been summoned to this place. Stunned, she listened to the story of her daughter and the peddler man; bewildered because she had never before heard of any such incident and knew nothing of what he was talking about and astonished because Alison had apparently confessed to being a witch. None of this made any sense to her. Nowell saw her confusion and continued.

"Are you a witch, madam?" he asked sharply

Elizabeth said nothing.

"Are any members of your family practiced in the black arts?"

Still no answer came.

"Look, Mrs Device" Nowell's voice was hushed and deeper than before "your daughter has told me everything. There is little point in saying nothing"

Elizabeth looked him straight in the face. Alison had told

him everything – what did that mean? What was this 'everything' of which he spoke?

Had her second child betrayed her kin? The only thing Elizabeth knew for sure was that there would be some questions asked when she got home.

But before then she had to get through this.

Nowell pressed on with his questions.

"I hear that your family are prone to skin conditions Mrs Device. Is that correct?"

"Skin conditions sir? No sir not as I am aware.

My mother has but one blemish upon her skin, but she is the only one sir"

"One blemish?" Nowell probed further, "of what kind?" "Just a blue mark, on her left side sir, like a bruise some'd say but for that it has been there for all of my lifetime I'm sure. I think it's been there since birth sir. It's just a blotch sir, nowt neither more nor less than that".

Nowell allowed a brief, sly smile to cross his lips. She had fallen for his trick; of course he had heard nothing of her family and any skin complaints, he had made that part up in order to gain a response – and it had worked. He needed to see this blemish for himself, somehow.

Elizabeth saw his smirk and was quietly alarmed.

She would not answer any more of his questions, she decided, for she refused to incriminate either herself or her family, nor surrender her loved ones at any cost. She shuffled slightly on the spot and tried to hold her nerve.

Eventually Nowell lost patience with her silence and dismissed her from the room, calling forth instead her son, one James Device.

Minutes later a tall spindly youth trudged into the room. Nowell looked at the dishevelled sight that appeared before him; his shirt ripped and boots hole- ridden and covered with dry, crusted mud, and cringed. The boy however, just looked ahead of him, his eyes blinking incessantly.

"Are you James Device?" Nowell began.

The question was greeted with a decisive nod of the head.

"Welcome to my house James" Nowell smiled. James' hands began to twitch as he rubbed his middle finger vigorously between the opposite thumb and index finger.

"Like it 'ere" he replied, gazing about him almost vacantly. "Pretty house this. Smells nice too".

"Thank you James. Now, I am going to ask you some questions, if that is alright with you?"

Again James nodded his head, his mop of black hair falling untidily around his face.

"James" Nowell whispered "do you know what magic is?"

James looked up in excitement; he knew the answer to this question.

"Aye sir, I knows what magic is. Magic is spells

and curses" his voice quickened with enthusiasm, his joy increased even more so as the older man confirmed his answer.

"Yes James, that's right. Tell me boy, have you ever met anyone who used magic?"

James pursed his lips and raised his eyes to the ceiling.

"All is well boy, I am very interested in magic and would like to meet the people who use it" Nowell explained. He wasn't lying, he thought to himself, for he *was* interested in such people – the boy didn't need to know why.

"Aye sir" James continued, reassured "I knows some folks who do magic sir".

"Are you sure? Have you *seen* them do it?"

"Aye sir. Many a time sir. "

Nowell leaned forward in his seat, his hands clasped together in anticipation. This boy was simple, that was clear, and he was certain of success in his interrogation. All he needed was for James to talk – and he would, Nowell was sure.

"Is Chattox one of those people?"

"Aye sir, she's a witch sir – and not a nice one neither. She n' her folks are nowt but trouble."

"Interesting" Nowell stroked his chin. "And what of your grandmother; is she one?"

James continued to rub his finger, his pale yellow teeth chewed at his bottom lip.

"Imagine boy, your own grandmother a witch. How much fun would that be? I guess no one would dare to cause you trouble if they knew there was magic in the family. Think how wonderful that would be".

James' eyes sparkled with delight. At last someone might think his family were wonderful, or at least better than they were regarded at present. Clapping his hands together eagerly, a toothy grin spread across his face, he began to tell Nowell everything.

10

Less than an hour later Nowell called the mother and son back into the room. As they stood before him, the deformed middle aged woman and the simple young boy, he knew what he had to do. He didn't like it – didn't like it at all – but he had no choice. He had to let them go.

"Well Mrs Device, Master Device" he began, clearing his throat with a low grunting cough.

"I thank you for your help today. You have been most cooperative. I now have much of the information that I need to finish my work; well almost, at least. You may now go home".

His guests glanced at each other with hardly a movement of their heads.

"You can go" Nowell repeated with a smile.

"Oh thank you sir, thank you so much" Elizabeth almost screeched as the words rushed off her tongue. Stooping her aching frame in an awkward attempt at a curtsey she grabbed her son's arm and whisked him towards the door.

Suddenly she stopped. A sudden thought had entered her head; what about Alison? Was she free to go home too?

"Mr Nowell, sir" she began cautiously, "what has

happened to my daughter?"   `

Nowell turned to face her once more. He had almost forgotten about the young girl whose reckless actions had brought them here. Setting his glass down on the table, he peered over the rim of his spectacles and muttered quietly

"No Mrs Device, your daughter must remain here for a while".

Elizabeth bowed her head and closed her eyes. She had no idea what his answer meant, but even to her it did not sound good. With a small nod of acknowledgement she thanked him once more and made her exit.

As mother and son trudged wearily through the rain-soaked grass not a word was spoken between them. Both stared intently ahead: James silently gleeful that he had been of use to someone at last, and Elizabeth thinking dolefully of the child she had left behind. What was to become of Alison now? The poor child – she had done nothing wrong and now… Elizabeth shook her head and tried to dislodge the thoughts. She didn't know why Alison had had to remain behind, but she was certain that this – whatever it was – was just a mistake. A big mistake. Her child would be home in the morning.

But Alison did not return in the morning.

She didn't return at any point in the next day.

The remaining members of the Device household sat around the withering fire and watched the night encroach around them. They had eaten nothing since the previous morning before the meeting at Ashlar House, for the provision of food was Alison's chore; and besides, no one else was fit for the task. Their stomachs rumbled with the emptiness of hunger. Something scampered across the floor, its shadow towering above them in the dying flickers of the flames. It was a rat. James watched it as it explored its surroundings and couldn't help but wonder what it might taste like to his grumbling stomach. The creature must have sensed his surveillance for it stopped suddenly and stared at him, its blood red eyes shining in the darkness, before turning quickly away and retreating out of the hole- ridden wooden door. James sighed and returned his attentions to his dreams. It was the youngest Device who broke the silence.

"When is Alison coming home?"

Nobody spoke; the three older people casting glances between themselves in a silent admission that none knew what to reply.

"She'll be home when she's home" the grandmother

answered sharply "now take yeself off to bed and be gone with ye".

The child began to mumble with disagreement over the command, her almost inaudible complaints meeting with a stinging slap across the ear from the mother sitting to her side.

"Do as ye are told and with no arguing child" she was warned with a glance that told her to speak no more. Sulkily she retreated into the shadows and made for her bed.

With the child safely out of the room, the conversation turned to Alison for the first time since leaving Nowell's house the day before.

"Did ye know of this business with the peddler?" Elizabeth spoke into the gloom. The words echoed through the room as though unsure of to whom it was addressed. No matter for silence was all that greeted it.

"She'll be home soon enough" the grandmother laid a bony hand on her daughter's shoulder. "She ain't done wrong to no one and that's for sure. Alison's a good lass she is and they'll see that. God will make sure on it".

"What's God ever done for th' likes of us mother?" Elizabeth sighed.

"God doesn't like witches". Both women turned, almost startled, in the direction of the voice. In the stillness both had almost forgotten James was there.

"Whatever are you talking about boy?" Elizabeth spoke sternly to her only son.

"Alison's no witch".

"She is ma. You know she is. She cursed that peddler man and he fell down sick. They say he nearly died ma. Alison did that, with magic"

Elizabeth sat like a gargoyle in her seat, her long fingernails digging mercilessly into the flesh on the palm of her hand as her fists clenched ever more tightly at her side.

"That's enough James" she hissed, spitting out the words, "Don't be so silly!"

"Its not silly ma" James continued in complete ignorance of his mother's warning.

"And there was that thing with Henry Bulcock's lass. Alison cursed her, like she did the peddler man, just because she called her a witch."

"ENOUGH" Elizabeth's voice reached screeching pitch, "nothing came of the Bulcock girl, she's alive and well and making a nuisance of herself as much as she were before and no mistake. I hope you didn't go tellin' all o'this to hisnibs at the big house, there's enough trouble as it is".

James fell quiet and stared hard at the dying fire. Although he said nothing, his silence spoke volumes. Suddenly he felt a sharp pain as his mother's rough hand connected with the back of his head – once, twice and an even more brutal third time.

"You fool" she yelped, "what have ye done?

What HAVE ye done?" the pitch of her voice rising still further as it increased in volume.

Without waiting for an answer from her dumbstruck son she swirled her plump body around and stomped off up the stairs.

James slumped in his seat, his hand clasped tightly to the side of his head as though trying to protect himself from the blows; unsuccessfully as it turned out as a fourth one hit him like a thunderbolt.

"Dim-witted boy" he heard his grandmother whisper in his ear.

Leaning forward and holding his head between the palms of his hands, James rocked back and forth and sobbed inconsolably as he was left alone in the shadows and embers. What *had* he done? – he didn't understand. He had told the truth to the important man in the big house; the man who was interested in his family, in *him*, what was wrong with that? Alison is a witch, that was what everyone was saying; he had never seen her use magic, but that didn't mean she couldn't, did it? The nice man wanted to know about magic, she was in no danger; he would ask his questions and then let her go, James was sure of it. And his family, well they would become famous because of him. His mother and grandmother wouldn't be quite so mean then, would they?

And with that thought he laid his tear and mud stained face down on a mound of straw, curled into a ball and cried himself to sleep.

11

Two days later they came again.

The horse and cart trudged its way up the old dirt path and pulled to a stop outside its destination. Two well dressed gentlemen climbed carefully over the side, their solemn faces betraying their disgust as they connected with the mud and puddle strewn ground. Without a word they headed for the building and hit the door with an authoritative knock. The door opened almost immediately, the face of a dirty small child peering around its frame.

"Morning" one of the men said sternly. "We are here to see your grandmother"

The child made no answer, staring blankly at them through wide brown eyes.

"Is she at home?" the other man added, slightly unnerved by her gaze.

Silently the child stepped to one side and pulled the creaky door with her. The two men stepped inside and looked distastefully at the sight before them; the floor was covered with an uneven carpet of straw, the furniture – what little there was – was discoloured and full of holes and one of the men was sure he had just seen a rat in the distance. He shuddered at the very idea. Still, they had a job to do.

"Ma" the child yelled, "there's two menfolk to see grandmother"

"What do they want?" a voice replied from the back of the house.

"I told ye, they want Grandmother" the child shouted back.

"Don't show me yer cheek child or I'll show thee me hand"

The stout frame of Elizabeth Device appeared through the door opposite, rubbing her soil stained hands together roughly. She looked suspiciously at the suited gentlemen standing in her living room before waving a hand in their direction as an invitation to take a seat. The men respectfully declined the offer. Elizabeth shrugged and looked them up and down; she had seen one of them before, she was sure of it – she just couldn't quite remember where.

"What do ye want with my mother?" she asked sharply.

Before either man could give her an answer, an elderly woman entered from behind her, her wooden stick making dull thudding sounds on the almost bare floor.

"Leave them be Lizzie" the old woman snapped

"Now, what would fine folk like you want wi' the likes of me?"

"Are ye called by the name of Elizabeth Southern, Madam?" the man shuffled his feet as he asked the question.

"Aye. What of it?"

The man cleared his throat with a sharp cough before continuing.

"Then madam, you must come with us immediately"

Elizabeth Southern made no movement.

"Must?" she repeated, "on whose say so?"

"Mr Nowell Madam."

The younger Elizabeth pricked up her ears at the mention of the name. What did Nowell want with her mother? Swallowing the urge to speak up and ask such questions, she returned to her task and allowed the conversation to continue.

"And who is this Mr Nowell, may I ask?" the elderly woman persisted, although in truth she knew exactly whom this person was, and what he wanted with her.

"The magistrate madam" came the reply.

Elizabeth Southern hummed knowingly to herself for a moment before taking a step forward, stumbling slightly on an out-of-place pile of straw. One of the men kindly reached out a strong arm to prevent her from falling, to which she meekly gave thanks and the excuse that her eyes no longer worked as they used to be. In truth her eyes no longer worked at all.

Regaining her balance, she gripped tightly onto her stick and hobbled towards the door, out into the bright early spring morning and allowed herself to be lifted gently onto the awaiting cart. Seconds later the horses, the cart and its new passenger disappeared down the hillside and out of view. Her daughter watched them go and thought of her own child, who was still in the custody of that Nowell man – at least as far as she knew. Turning, she made her way back into her home and pushed the door closed behind her. Not for the first time all she could do now was sit and wait.

12

Journey completed, the aged woman was guided to a seat in the waiting area at Ashlar House and asked politely, but firmly to wait. Stick resting on the edge of the chair she rubbed a long, bony hand across the furnishings – back and forth almost longingly. She had no idea what material any of it was, but it felt lovely just the same. If only she could have such beautiful things in her home; but that was never likely and certainly never will be now. Folks such as her live in a different world to that of the man in whose house she now sat, old Elizabeth knew that. She sighed deeply and continued her musings.

"Mrs Southern" the deep voice brought her suddenly out of her thoughts and back into the room.

"Aye sir" she responded.

"Please step this way madam"

Elizabeth pulled herself slowly to her feet, grimacing under the pain of rheumatism and other ailments of her years.

"'This way' ain't no good for those of us who cant see, boy" she stated, fumbling for her stick.

"Sorry madam" he mumbled apologetically, taking her

gently by the arm.

"I'll lead you, shall I?"

"That be very kind of you sir" Elizabeth bowed her head in thanks. Together they set off down the corridor.

"Do ye know why I am called hither?" she enquired.

Her companion shook his head.

"No madam" he added urgently, remembering her lack of vision. "I'm sure I do not, although all shall become clear very soon".

"I'm sure it will boy" she half laughed. "I'm sure it will".

"Ah" another voice boomed out as the pair made their way through a large doorway.

"Thank you Bennett" Nowell dismissed her guide, who bowed and made his exit.

"Now then" Nowell began as the door was shut firmly on them.

"You must be Mrs Southern".

"That I am sir. That I am!"

"Mrs *Elizabeth* Southern?"

"That's me sir"

"Tell me, are you also called by the name of Demdike?"

Elizabeth's lips pursed sullenly. She was as aware of the name by which she was commonly referred, as she was the meaning behind it.

"Aye sir! I do believe they call me such"

"Tell me, madam. Are you aware of the meaning of the word Demdike?"

The look on her face told him that she did.

"Are you aware Madam that the name Demdike means "demon woman"?

Elizabeth made no reply.

"Mrs Southern, I shall get to the point"

"I wish that ye would" she retorted. Nowell smirked to himself, and pushed his spectacles back up his nose.

"Indeed. Madam, I have heard tell that you are practiced in the dark arts. Do you have anything to say with regard to such matters?"

Elizabeth tapped the end of her stick with her finger, the sound barely audible in the huge space of the room. Nowell scratched his head.

"You see Mrs Southern" he continued, an idea suddenly coming to him

"I have recently been talking to a friend of yours; a Mrs Anne Whittle".

"That witch ain't no friend of mine" Demdike hissed, her hand coiling tightly around the body of her stick. Nowell knew he had hit the spot.

"Mrs Southern" he paused "I am going to be honest with you. I have been hearing tales about Mrs Whittle and I think you might be able to help, but you must tell me the truth."

Demdike heard the words and she liked them. She liked them a lot. Chattox was in possible trouble and she, Elizabeth, was needed to help keep her there. Nothing would give her greater pleasure.

"Mrs Southern" Nowell paused "do you believe it is possible to kill a person by magic?"

"Has been known sir"

"Do you know how it is possible?"

Demdike hesitated, choosing her words with care.

"Tell me Madam, what do you know of clay images?"

A broad smile blazoned across Demdike's face. Did she know about the use of clay? Of course she did; so did Chattox, and she was going to make sure Nowell knew that too.

"Have you ever seen Mrs Whittle with anything like the clay images of which you are clearly aware?"

"Aye sir" Demdike began, "twas just before young Nutter passed, to be sure"

"You mean Robert Nutter, of Greenhead?"

"Aye sir. About a half year before he passed. I saw a pair of folks in West Close. Of course me eyes were better then and I could make out the clay images they had wi' 'em; three of 'em sir – well two finished and one almost done. "

"What is the purpose of these images madam?"

"Why to cause the body to suffer sir!" Demdike tried to add an air of disdain to her words in attempt to persuade Nowell of her innocence in such doings.

"And you think there was a connection between what you saw and the death of Robert Nutter?"

"To be sure sir" Demdike nodded "for they were images of the Nutters"

Nowell studied her intently. She seemed convinced of her words but he could feel that she was holding something back. He needed her information, but he knew that wasn't going to be easy. He needed to put his guest at ease.

"Mrs Southern" he said in a low, calm voice.

"You're not in any trouble. My interest lays solely in Mrs Whittle and her activities. Anything else you tell me will be in the strictest confidence. I have spoken to a number of other people who have provided very useful information".

There was a moment of silence as both considered their next move.

"I've heard…" Nowell looked at her out of the corner of his eye, hoping a different approach may yield the results he was hoping for.

"That Mrs Whittle is the greatest witch in these parts".

Demdike once more began to tap the end of her stick, her thin lips pursed outwards as though insulted by his remarks.

"Humph" she allowed herself to say aloud.

"She's a witch, that's to be sure. As to being the greatest witch, well that remains to be seen sir"

Nowell smirked to himself and looked down at the pile of papers on the desk before him. He had hit the spot and he knew it.

"But then, some say that your powers are far greater than hers. Tell me Madam, which is correct?"

"Her powers are nothin' sir, for any fool wi'

a base know of magic can turn ale sour or

make ill a sheep" Demdike spoke the words with scarcely

contempt.

"So, Mrs Southern, you believe that magic does exist and that there are people who use its powers for their own reasons?"

Demdike allowed a small chuckle to escape her thin lips.

"People claim that magic is dead, or worse; that it's not real" she began. "That's simply not true. Magic, Mr Nowell, is a beast. It feeds on blood, on death, and then it returns to sleep until the hunger awakes it again. In answer to your question sir, magic is very much real and folks like us use it in many ways; some good, some not so good. We're not all bad folk sir. All depends on th' folks themsels".

And with that, the interview was ended.

13

Roger Nowell leaned back into his armchair and ran a rough hand over his face; his silver rimmed spectacles perched on the summit of his head. On his knee sat the notebook in which he had furiously scribbled down the words of the people whose futures he possibly now held in his grasp, along with a now unsealed letter he had received that morning. Slowly he traced a hand over the spider-scrawled letters of the word 'father' and exhaled deeply, his mind racing with images of his eldest son. He could see him clearly in his mind – the small dark haired child with his even darker plate like eyes, looking up at him with pure admiration in his face. Of the surviving six of the ten offspring that he had brought into this world, he had loved this boy - his first born -most dearly, and was most proud of the clever and handsome young man that he had become. Or he had been, until recent events had overtaken them. Now his pride had been dashed, and the future – for both himself and his son – was far from certain.

Nowell picked up the notebook and stared at it unblinkingly, his grasp on its smooth edges tightening slowly as one question repeated in his head; could the contents of that book hold an answer to the problem? He was beginning to think so.

But were these people, the poor, wretched creatures that had stood in that very office that day, *really* witches? Nowell wasn't too sure. He had heard the tales of witchcraft that floated around the area, although he had not investigated any of them in any great detail until this moment; indeed he had dismissed most of them as pure hearsay, as had many other knowledgeable people that he knew. But this time it was different. He had met the supposed possessors of these malevolent powers; he had heard their voices above the roar of common opinion. He had listened intently to all sides of this potent dispute, the accusations and hatred that spilled out from each of the parties involved, yet he was still unconvinced – of either guilt or innocence.

His eyes wandered around the room, fixing on nothing until they came to rest on the portrait on the wall above his desk. The dark eyes burrowed into his flesh, he could feel his skin burning under their gaze until he could stand it no longer and was forced to avert his eyes. Still the sensation persisted, smouldering deeper and deeper into his being. Nowell shuddered in his seat. He had never met the man in the picture – men such as he were not worthy to be accepted into the presence of the king too often – and yet somehow he could hear his voice in his head.

"Punish them" the voice echoed.

"Evil must not be allowed to flourish in this realm!"

Nowell threw his head back against the chair and breathed in deeply, allowing the air to once more escape his pursed lips with a single slow, lingering push. He must have been sitting there for quite some time he noted, for a pencil grey darkness was setting in beyond the window and feint shadows crept along the panelled walls. It was unusually humid for a March evening, of which he was glad for he had no desire to call in a maid to stoke up the fireplace. Slowly he pulled himself to his feet and lit the candle, its orange flame dancing ominously against its black background. Nowell stared into the glow and wondered silently what the flames of Hell looked like, for he could well see that particular road opening up before him – either for these wretched souls he was being called upon to condemn as creatures of the devil, or for himself should they be innocent of such crimes. But he could not think that way; he *would* not allow it. He had a job to do and, one way or another, he had to act. He had to save his child from the accusations against him, or at least divert attention from them.

Wearily he began to pace the room; back and forth over the freshly polished floorboards, hardly noticing the slight squeak that radiated every so often from beneath his feet. He had never been a big believer in prayer but he suddenly found his lips moving in a silent appeal to God for deliverance from this unbearable burden. If he was up there, Nowell imagined, he must help him now. After making a few more lengths of the room he returned to the desk and picked up the book that lay there; it was the Bible – the new one commissioned by the King himself only a year earlier. The leather cover smelt like new, indeed it was almost stiff as though it had hardly ever been opened. In truth it hadn't for he was not too interested in matters of religion as a rule. Pulling it towards him he opened it, smoothed down the wavering pages with his hand and began to skim the somewhat tiny print that lay there. Suddenly his eyes struck upon one sentence that appeared to jump out of the page at him – he read the eight words repeatedly: *"Thou shalt not suffer a WITCH to live"*.

The words sank slowly into his head; *Thou shalt not suffer a WITCH to live.* That was it. The answer, the precedent was immediately before his eyes. God had provided him with a way, he *had* to take it. There was no other option.

14

The horse and cart made its way through the narrow, winding streets, its wheels bouncing noisily over the cobbles as the first signs of daylight emerged over the hill. It had stopped first at the home of Mother Demdike and her family shortly following the call of the cockerel in the yard, the old woman having been bundled into the back with nothing but the tattered clothing that hung around her body and told to maintain her silence. And so it was that it made its way now to collect its next passengers; old Chattox and her daughter Anne.

They were collected at their door by the driver- a rough looking man with a long pointed nose and short beard which looked for all the world to be somehow connected to the stained and hole-ridden ruff that surrounded his thick neck – while his companion sat guard of their already in situ passenger. Demdike wondered whether he really imagined that she would make an attempt at escape, her being over eighty years in age and not in the best of health, yet still he watched her eagerly ready to pounce should the opportunity present itself. She smiled beneath her cap and snuggled further into her seat.

"Shove up" the gruff voice of the driver addressed her.

"Make room for yer friends".

Demdike raised her head to look at them, but made no attempt to move her frail body even an inch from where she sat.

"Ain't no friend o' mine" she croaked, extending a bony finger in the direction of her nemesis.

"All hell and the power of Satan himsel' will freeze afore I share room wi that".

With that she closed her eyes once more.

"Ye think that we seek yer company, ye old crow" Chattox replied
"why id sooner walk te gallows meself".

"Off ye go then" Demdike retorted, not even bothering to open her eyes on this occasion

"An' may th' devil tek ye".

"Now now, ladies. Play nicely"

The driver and his companion grinned at each other, a look of mischief in their eyes.

"Now shove up and let 'em get in"

Still Demdike refused to move, indeed she remained staunchly in her fixed position until the bearded man lost all patience and moved her himself, the doing of which earned him a short sharp rebuke from the stubborn old woman. The two other women were then hoisted into the cart and they were once more on their way.

Hardly a word was spoken from thence forth, aside from the occasional curse from one or other of the passengers when the cart hit a rough stretch of pathway, or if their uncomfortable shuffling caused them to make contact with one of their companions. At one point Demdike's crooked old walking stick caught the back of Chattox's bony leg, earning its owner a moment of abuse from the victim. Demdike made no response. The cart rumbled on through the early spring countryside, stopping occasionally for the odd sheep that had strayed from its field, or the deer that roamed the area at will as the seconds turned to minutes, the minutes into hours. Birds hovered and swooped above the cargo, hoping for scraps of food that never came. People came out of the dilapidated houses that lay scattered at intervals across the route, interested to see what was making the noise that echoed around in the emptiness. They looked away as the cart passed them, not one of them wishing to look the passengers in the face. They knew who they were; the rumours had spread across Pendle like the wind, the suggestion of witchcraft too scandalous to be ignored. The three infamous faces in the rear of the cart told them the stories were true; Demdike, Chattox and their families had been taken into custody. No one was in doubt of their guilt – the only surprise was that it had taken so long.

They rode on through the morning and into the

early afternoon, the three women staring expressionlessly out at their surroundings as though they had been there numerous times before, although not one of them had ever ventured this far away from home in the entirety of their lives. Nothing seemed to penetrate their vacant stares, not even the occasional colourful butterfly that fluttered past their faces or the array of wild flowers that littered the edges of the path and the fields beyond. Throughout the whole of their passage their faces remained, set as stone against the gaping uncertainty that lay ahead of them.

At length the cart turned a sharp corner and their destination came into view, the great stone keep looming menacingly above them as they made their approach, the bump of the cobbles bringing the party firmly back to reality of their situation. Each of the women eyed their new location warily as the horses were pulled to a heavy stop on the cobbled pathway. Their host jumped effortlessly from his seat, patted the animals tenderly on their bulging necks, whispered a few inaudible words in their ears and strode casually towards his human cargo.

"Reight there ladies" he beamed,

"Here we are at last. Down ye get now".

He reached out a thick, dirty brown hand in the direction of the youngest passenger, who grasped it tightly between her palms and accepted his help with her dismount. She was too thin and gaunt to be considered a beauty he noted, and her age was almost indeterminable beneath the dirty wrinkled complexion, although he would wager a day's pay that she was over half a century old at the least. He wrinkled up his nose as she neared him. She *smelled* like she had lived for half a century. Lived, and never washed.

Old Chattox disembarked next, refusing calmly to take the driver's hand and stumbling uncertainly onto the cobbles. Her daughter caught her arm as she lost her balance.

"Yer a good lass ye are" Chattox patted the supporting hand.

"Ye look affa yer old ma well ye do".

The two women huddled together beneath the shadow of the keep, the daughter protecting the mother with a strong arm as they awaited their next move. The driver checked their well-being and turned his attention to the last of his passengers.

Demdike remained seated in her slouched position in the back of the cart, her shawl wrapped firmly around her shoulders and her once-white cap pulled down over her eyes. He held out his hand as he had done for the two who had gone before. Demdike made no attempt to move. The driver almost thought she had fallen asleep. He crept closer, heaving his heavy body onto the side of the cart, and reached out a hand. Suddenly she jolted into life, pushing his hand away with such force that it thudded painfully onto the wooden frame of the vehicle. It was all he could do to stop himself crying out with pain as he withdrew his hand and shook it vigorously.

"Take yer hands off me" the old woman hissed.

"I ain't going nowhere until I know where it is ye hav' brung us to".

"This ma'am" the driver said dryly "this is the old castle at Clitheroe".

"I ain't goin' in no castle, be it in Clitheroe or that blasted hole called London" Demdike retorted firmly, still refusing to move from her position.

"You ain't got no choice" the man snapped, grabbing at her now flailing arm. It was a struggle but he eventually managed to pull the elderly woman down from the cart.

"There ye go" he addressed a group of men who had strolled casually yet smartly down the path to meet them. "They're all yers now".

Each of the three men grabbed one of the weary travellers by the arm and, with little care for the effects of age and infirmity, marched them back up the steep, unlevelled path towards the castle. The driver watched until they rounded the slight bend that occurred halfway, at which point he hoisted himself back onto his seat behind the increasingly impatient horses, steered them around and, without a backward glance, went on his way.

They spent only one cold, everlasting night in the castle, huddled together in a corner of the small square room into which they had been hastily ushered and abandoned. The next morning they were once more on the move.

15

Malkin Tower sat alone in a large field somewhere in the middle of the vast abyss that was the Pendle countryside, with nothing for miles at either side, and only the brooding slope of the hill behind. So far removed was it from everywhere that it was almost like it was in its own world, its own reality; the nearest neighbours were at least a mile away, the market even further and the chances of any sort of socialising were very remote. In some ways Jennet Device was glad of the seclusion, particularly that morning as she ran through the fields, the soft mud splattering her bare feet and up her legs as she battled through the gangs of wild flowers and long grass. Every now and then she turned partially to cast a timid glance over her shoulder at the group behind her; they were quite a distance away, yet seemed to be gaining ground on her quickly no matter how fast she ran. On reaching the old wooden stile Jennet launched herself over it with ease and took refuge behind a gorse bush, her breath catching as it made its rapid escape from her body. A short while later the group arrived at the stile. They made no attempt to cross the divide; the territory beyond was alien to them, not to mention unfriendly. It was *her* world and they had no desire to go there. They stood in their group for a moment, looking puzzled as to where their prey could have vanished to, before growing bored of their game and heading back in the direction they had just come.

"Wonder if she's gone to find her favver?" one of them spoke loudly as they turned, as though sure that Jennet was still close enough to hear their jibes.

"Doubt it" chimed another, "even her mam don't know who *he* is".

Jennet's heart sank. She had heard such things all her life, in various forms, but they cut deeper with every occurrence. Breathing deeply she tried to resist the urge to reveal herself and give them a piece of her mind; aside from the fact that they were bigger than her, and that there were more of them, Jennet knew they were right. The only person who knew the identity of Jennet's father was her mother – and she was not for telling. Jennet curled her small hand into a tight fist at her side, her fingernails burrowing into her palm as she waited for the group to disappear completely into the distance. Slowly she pulled herself out of the bush, kicked a patch of daisy flowers in frustration and began to trudge home.

As she came within sight of the ramshackle building that she called home Jennet could feel the anger fluttering around her stomach. She had often wondered about her nameless father, had often questioned various family members as to what they knew about him, but had always been met with either silence or an icy glare that strongly suggested that she probe no further. Sometimes when she lay down at night she would try to picture him; what he looked like, what he did, where he was. In her head he had been a gentleman – perhaps a judge, maybe even someone very important like a Lord or a Baron. He had had to keep his distance all her life to avoid a scandal that would have ruined him. Maybe he had been called to do some kind of service in a different area and had not been able to keep in touch, even though he had very much wanted to. Another time he had been a peddler man, or a farmer. Perhaps he had been a neighbour. Whatever he had been, there was one thing that he wasn't. He wasn't there. Slowly she crossed the field and ducked under the wooden gate that lay at the boundary of the Malkin enclosure. She could see her brother outside the house, his long coat trailing around him like the vestments of a clergyman as he moved a pile of wood from one place to another. He didn't look up as she approached, although she was sure that he was aware of her presence. "Ey up James" she half smiled. "Where's ma?" "Inside" he answered gruffly, still not acknowledging the child.

"She ain't in a good temper right na, mind". Jennet made no reply. There was nothing more to say, therefore he continued battling with the firewood and left his sister to make her way into the house. Elizabeth Device was in the sitting room, if a shabby room with only one chair could be referred to as a sitting room. She was seated on a hay bale by the window, staring unflinchingly at the empty rocking chair next to the fire. Like her son before her, she too did not acknowledge that Jennet was there. The child sat on the floor at her mother's feet and laid her head against her strong, solid leg.

"Ma" Jennet began timidly following a few moments of nothingness. There was no response from behind her. Jennet pulled herself to her knees and leant her elbows on those of her mother.

"Ma, Who was ma favver?"

Suddenly Elizabeth rose to her feet, shrugging off the touch of her daughter who almost tumbled face first onto the floor as she did so. "What do ye need to know that fer?" she questioned, walking to the fireplace and piling some fresh wood onto the burnt embers.

"I just wondered" Jennet said quietly.

"Well don't wonder" she snapped. "That be the last thing to worry 'bout now. Ye wan' ta concern yeself with the kin ye have, and what trouble they be in".

Jennet dipped her head and stared at the floor, her face flushed. She so badly wanted to know about him, but perhaps now was not quite the time.

"When's Gramma comin' 'ome?" she whispered, "and Alison?"

"They'll be a fair kind'a lucky if they ever come 'ome" Elizabeth retorted.

"This is a like bit of trouble" James added from the doorway.

"And who's fault be that then?" his mother turned on him, "Who opened their mouth and let the devil's words spew forth?" Now it was James' turn to redden and turn his face away. This only seemed to infuriate his mother further. "If only yer sister had sense to hold her curses. If only ye had sense to keep yer mouth closed. If only..." Elizabeth didn't finish her sentence, heaving her plump frame into her mother's rocking chair and turning it to the fire. Both Jennet and James looked at each other and made their escape – one in the direction of the garden, the other to the upstairs room. There was little point staying put; once their mother was in her present state of mind she would be neither shifted nor spoken to. Upstairs Jennet threw herself down on her straw bed, buried her head in the coarse bedding and began to sob. The words of the unkind children in the fields swirled around her head; she had often being called illegitimate, a bastard, the seed of a whore - even James and Alison cast such terms in her direction whenever the mood or the situation suited them. They referred to their father, her mother's late husband, as *our* father - making certain the youngest family member was fully aware that '*our*' did not mean '*your*'. They had called her blacky - the different one. Jennet may have had the Device family name but she was, without doubt, the outsider. Jennet knew it. The whole world knew it. The tears fell thick and fast, dampening the straw beneath her head. Images floated in and out of her mind - her mother, grandmother, her unknown father. Alison and James were there too, locking her out of the house as they had often done and calling her names. How she hated them, all of them. One day they would regret treating her so badly. One day, when she was older, she would make them all pay.

16

"Tell me about the Nutters, Mrs Whittle". Roger Nowell leaned back in the chair and surveyed the elderly woman from head to toe and back again. Old Chattox shuffled slightly on the spot, the end of her walking stick tapping gently on the hard floor.

"What about em?" She croaked.

"I hear you have had a small amount of trouble with them over the years" Nowell continued, his eyes never wavering.

"That lot be nowt but trouble" Chattox hissed, "each an every one of em".

Nowell was intrigued. He had been made fully aware of the accusations made by various members of the Nutter family against Mrs Whittle and her like, but it now appeared there may be grievances in the opposite direction too. Nowell loved a good neighbourly enmity, his nosiness and ear for gossip proving extremely useful in his profession. He had an ear for scandal, and it was beginning to burn.

"I believe there was a problem pertaining to some

land not too long ago" Nowell pressed on.

"Aye" Chattox agreed, "but tha' were nowt to do wi' me nor any o'mine".

"Indulge me" Nowell smirked, forgetting for a moment that his wry smile was lost on the blind old woman. Moments passed in awkward silence and Nowell began to grow impatient and decided on a different line of interrogation.

"Mrs Whittle did Robert Nutter and your daughter have some form of altercation at your home some time before he passed on?"

"Aye sir" she said stoutly, "but it were all 'is doin' mind. Not our Annie's, that's fer sure".

Nowell raised his eyebrows, smelling the onset of new, possibly vital information.

"What was?" he asked with a deliberate, if not exaggerated air of innocence.

"Why, he tried to lay hands on 'er, so he did. He comes to our home and makes suggestions that weren't proper sir – that arr not decent, even for the likes of us! My Annie's not that kind a' girl sir".

Nowell nodded his head.

"Of that I am sure Mrs Whittle" he said calmly,

"But these are serious accusations that you make against Mr Nutter. You must be sure that you are correct in what you say".

The old woman stiffened. Nowell could hear her inhale deeply as she considered her response. Blind as she was, even she could see the meaning in his words. People didn't take kindly to the 'her sort' making such talk about their betters, particularly in the absence of anything resembling evidence; and she had none of that. It would be their word against that of the Nutters, and there was precious little hope of anyone taking their part. Yet it had to be said; if only in this moment, in this room, those words would find their voice.

"Oh I am sure sir" she said firmly after swallowing hard,

"I belee' my girl o'er him any time sir. I bring my childer up proper so I did, so as they know not to tell untruths sir. We may not have had much to our name sir but I could give them that".

"Of course Mrs Whittle" Nowell tried to soothe the growing agitation in her voice.

"No one is suggesting that you didn't. I merely meant that such things can be easily…how can I put it... misinterpreted."

Chattox snorted loudly but made no attempt at reply; there was little point for she could see that this man was like all the others. Well he could believe what he wanted

"Hmmm. Tell me Mrs Whittle, have you ever been approached, by anyone, with a request to harm a member of the Nutter family, previous to this I mean?"

Chattox stiffened; she knew exactly to what Nowell was referring. She hesitated for a moment.

"Well sir, I tell from yer tone that ye know about old Lizzie Nutter. Indeed sir, she asked that we may bring about the end of her son, although we didn't do owt about it."

"We?" asked Nowell, nonchalantly.

"Mysel and three others whom I shall not name 'ere sir, if ye don't mind."

"Of course". The names of the others were not of great importance at that moment for they would add nothing to what he needed.

"Tell me Mrs Whittle, why would Mrs Nutter wish for the death of her own son?"

"For the land sir. With him dead the land would belong to the women folk, and that's all they care 'bout sir".

"And was Mrs Southern involved in this?"

For the first time Chattox looked visibly surprised.

"No sir, old Demdike had no part in this, at least not as far as I remember".

"And you say that nothing was ever done in regards to this matter?"

"No sir, for we would have nowt to do we' it. We are respectable folks sir".

Nowell tried desperately to suppress a smile. He knew a lot of people who would be thought of as respectable, but Chattox and her family were not amongst their number. The Nutters however fit very compactly into that social standing and, try as he might – although he was not inclined to try very hard – he simply could not take the word of this miserable wretch of a woman over that of her superiors. The land issue was perfectly plausible, for such possession was the mainstay of a life outside the grasp of poverty, but to request the destruction of your own child in pursuit of it was more than Roger Nowell was able to comprehend, especially as a father himself. But families can be a strange affair he told himself; many of the cases he had heard as a Justice over the years had taught him that, and there was just no telling what was hidden behind the doors of other people's houses. Nor was it any business of his, unless the law had been broken. The problem in the case of the tales of Pendle witchcraft was whether any laws *had* been broken, and how to prove it that they had. It was a thorny situation to say the least.

"Returning to the matter of the incident at your house, Mrs Whittle" Nowell continued, remembering the old woman who stood before him, her lips endlessly moving in almost silent chattering.

"Tell me again what happened".

Immediately the chattering ceased and Chattox pursed her tight, thin lips together. She had no desire to answer these questions; not because the subject was false for it was as true as she was standing there, but because she had a feeling that she knew where this was heading.

"Mrs Whittle" Nowell's voice became suddenly sharper.

"Would you have me believe that Master Nutter made inappropriate advances towards your daughter, that he suddenly took ill and subsequently passed, and that there is *no* connection between the two?"

"Believe what you will sir!" came the muttered reply, "but ye will find nuffin to help ye!"

Nowell's dark eyes flashed in buried anger. He knew full well that he had no evidence of a connection between the two occurrences, and would have no easy time making such a case before the law. Clenching his fists to suppress his fury he summoned a castle guard and Chattox was returned to the gaol.

17

The day was fresh and the air still as James Device stole quickly along the gravel path and away from Malkin Tower, his head lowered and his body stooped forwards as though trying to conceal his presence. Occasionally he cast a furtive glance around him, his eyes darting rapidly from left to right to ensure that nobody was around to witness his departure as down the gradual slope of the hillside he went, his hole-ridden boots kicking the stones, leaping effortlessly over the tiny ripples of water and muddy puddles and keeping as close to the hedges and bushes as was possible. There was nobody about for the morning was still new and, being Good Friday, those who were risen were already at Church. That meant that he was free to conduct his business undisturbed.

He followed the path down to the Rough Lee and along the banks of the stream that flowed between that place and the village of Barley to the west, stopping at intervals to throw a stone into the quiet waters or to launch a bigger one at a passing bird. At Barley he left the stream and began the steep climb up to the New Church, taking a particular interest in the fields he passed along the way. None of them had what he was looking for. Suddenly he stopped, his eyes fastened on a small group of sheep that stood in the pasture to his left, their heads raised as though staring at something in the distance. Taking a few seconds to ensure that he was alone, he jumped quickly over the gate and headed in their direction.

Despite his cautious approach the animals sensed his presence and scattered in each and every direction, their loud bleating echoing through the silence. James lunged after them, his flagpole frame flailing ridiculously with every unsuccessful catch. More than once he landed in a heap on the grass or, more uncomfortably, in a hedgerow, his clothes becoming increasingly tattered and dirty by the minute and his face not to dissimilar, and he was still no nearer to seizing his prey. The sheep were far more agile than he and a good deal quicker. After falling for a fifth time into the churned up mud patches he remained seated and considered his options.

He was just about to admit defeat when he heard the sound of bleating behind him. Sure that all the animals had, by now, retreated to safety James pulled himself to his feet and stared around him. There was nothing to be seen, yet the noisc continued to echo around him. With careful tread he made his way across the field, his feet squelching in the newly surfaced mud, making his way around the perimeter hedges that formed the enclosure. Having scoured three of the sides with no success James was about to give up when there was a sudden movement in the foliage to his right. He took two steps towards it before stopping in his tracks, his mind debating what he might find when he reached that place. What if it *wasn't* a sheep in there? For all he knew it could be a fox, or a wolf, even a bear. His body began to tremble slightly as he considered his next move, until a moment of clarity cleared his mind and reminded him that any foxes that happened to be roaming the area would probably pay more attention to the vast number of hen coops that littered the area than they would a field full of sheep. Nobody had seen any wolves in Pendle for generations, perhaps even longer than that, and bears – well that was just foolish thinking. A bear wouldn't have been able to conceal itself in a hedge of that size anyhow. And besides, bears, wolves or foxes do not make that bleating noise he had heard so clearly. Shaking his shoulders in a bid to halt the trembles he concluded that it was, in all likelihood a sheep, and continued his steps forward, peeling the foliage apart with as much care and caution as his lumbering body would allow. It *was* a sheep; or to be more accurate – it was that day's dinner.

The creature lay on its side in the space, its head craned upwards as it locked eyes with its human predator. James could see the look of fear in its dark eyes, a menacing smirk spreading across his face as his hand reached inside the pocket of his jacket and pulled out a casing of rusted-brown leather. His eyes flickered as he released the blade from its sheath and held it up to the sun, the metal glistening in the morning light. Falling to his knees he grabbed the stricken creature by the head and sunk the knife into its tooth-white neck, the colour of which turned quickly into a deep red as the last signs of life were parted from the now still body. Within minutes James Device was making his way back the way he had travelled earlier that morning, his movements brisk despite the weighty sack upon his back and the regular drip of crimson falling like rain upon the path behind him. Still not a person was within sight, making his journey far less problematic than it could well have been had anyone stopped to ask what was in his pack. As it was, he made it back to Malkin as quietly as he had left it.

The house had seemingly sprung into life – or some semblance of it – for the old wooden door was wide open and he could see smoke wafting out of the chimney. That, James thought, was a sure sign that the breakfast fire had already been lit, although he had no idea as to what this 'breakfast' could have been, for food was one of the luxuries they could never afford.

The sound of raised voices rang from the gaping entrance; James assumed that his little sister was once again in some form of trouble.

"Get ye outta mi sight" his mother yelled over her shoulder as her plump frame appeared in the doorway. James heaved the slipping sack back up onto his shoulder and took three steps forward, a large tooth-filled grin spreading across his mud-spattered face.

"What 'ave ye got to grin about?" the woman snapped as he approached.

"We got vis'tors 'ere at dusk and nowt to give 'em, nor shall *we* eat again today. Ye and yer sister 'ave left us in a right muddle and no mistake. Now she's gone, ye grandmother's gone and I'm left 'ere with you useless pair of nothin's and less than nowt else. You tell me wat there is to grin about!"

James looked his mother straight in the face as e dropped the sack on the ground between them with a dull thud. She stared down at the delivery, with its rapidly spreading red stain and increasingly pungent smell, and then back up at her still beaming son.

"And what the deuce is that?" she said, a sharp suspicion penetrating her voice.

"I 'ope you ain't done nowt daft agin, ye hear?"

James shuffled on the spot and swallowed hard.

"Its dinner, Ma".

The old woman looked at him doubtfully and leaned forward to perform a closer inspection. pulling the neck of the sack open and immediately recoiling, if only for an instant.
"And where, may I ask, did you get hold of this" she hissed through the remainder of her pale yellow teeth.

"Barley way" James grinned, an air of obvious pride spread across his face.

His mothers stared at him for a moment, unsure of whether to hit or hug the boy. Eventually she decided on neither.

"Ah well, don't s'pose they'll miss it". she said, gripping the parcel shut within her fist. "Ye've dun well boy" she patted him on the chest, as she turned and headed back to the house, the cargo hauled unceremoniously over her shoulder, muttering the words " for once" beneath her breath. James, at the same time both surprised and delighted at the rare words of kindness from his parent, turned and slinked off back down the lane to see what else he could lay his hands on.

By the time he returned, his mother was rushing around the kitchen in a frenzy and
the house was filled with the smell of roasted lamb. Still grinning with the memory of his recent triumph, James stepped boldly over the threshold and moved towards the table.

"No ye don't" the woman half screeched, flapping at him with the piece of stiff material she had being using to handle the now cooked meat.

"That's not fer you, so it ain't. That's fer th' visters we got comin ere, not fer yer grubby mitts"

James quickly retracted his partially outstretched hand and returned it to his pocket.

"And get yer boots off, Yer traipsing muck through th' house" she continued, turning back to the meal.

"Jennet, don't just sit there like a church goblin, get that mud cleaned up".

Jennet looked up from where she was seated, an expression of indignant shock upon her face.

"It ain't my mess" she retorted, causing her parent to turn sharply and fling a large wooden spoon in her direction. Jennet ducked, the implement flying over her head and colliding with the wall with a thud.

"Curse ye child, will ye do nuffin that yer asked." She snarled.

"But *he* did it" Jennet gestured in the direction of her brother, who was pulling at his boot, trying to dislodge his grimy foot.

"Why should *I* clean it up."

"Because I said so, and if ye want feeding tonight then you'll do as yer bid, and be quick about it!"

"But..." Jennet began. She didn't get any further with her protest. The woman's face twisted into a devil like grimace, and her body began to shake with rage. She took two heavy steps towards her youngest child, who immediately knew that the argument was lost. Quickly she darted for the door and grabbed the handle of the old, slightly worse-for-wear broom. The mother had halted her advance the very second her daughter had moved, retaining her icy glare until certain that her bidding was being done.

"Next time ye'll be cleaning it up without the broom, if yer not careful" she snapped, turning back to the fire to stoke the flames until their shadows danced high on the walls. Wrinkling up her face, Jennet stuck out her short round-ended tongue at her mother's back, and continued to sweep the fresh mud backwards towards the open doorway. Suddenly something caught the back of her legs and she felt herself stumbling and falling to the ground, landing on her bottom on the hard ground.

Looking up she saw the face of her brother laughing with silent menace as he sat on the threshold cleaning his boots.

"Did that hurt ye, did it" he chuckled. "From now on ye do as ye are told, do ye hear?"

Jennet did hear, but she didn't answer her tormentor: her bottom was sore and she was almost sure she could feel blood on the back of her leg. She looked up at him, hurt and hate brimming within her heart, fresh warm tears within her eyes.

"Babby" he snarled, rising from his task and kicking her forcefully in the side as he stepped over her.

"Things are bad enough wi'out you mekking muvver mad, ye little rat"

Jennet said nothing as James stalked away, leaving her lying on the doorstep. There was little point in her doing so, for any response from her would have incurred an even harsher time, and no other effect whatsoever. No, Jennet would say nothing. She would bide her time.

18

Darkness began to fall, bringing with it a vast grey mist that shrouded the hill and its surroundings in a heavy gloom as Good Friday drew to a close. Jennet Device had been sent to bed early, and with none of the delicious feast that graced the kitchen downstairs being allowed to pass her half starved lips, while James had been told – in the most severe tone - to say nothing and leave his mother to do all the talking. That woman herself was now standing at the door awaiting the arrival of her visitors, her apron having been swilled in the well and dried before the fire, her wiry pencil coloured hair tied scraped tightly backwards into a bun that sat squarely on the top of her head. Every once in a while she turned inwards to ensure that the pot was not boiling over, or that neither of her remaining offspring were up to mischief while her back was turned before returning, briefly satisfied, to her vigil.

Eventually they came, one by one or in small groups as suited their own circumstances, each of them heading immediately towards the glowing grate in order to warm their hands before the raging flames. By the hour of eleven fourteen people were huddled in the tiny room of Malkin Tower, the younger ones seated on the floor, the elders given places upon the hay bales that Jemmy had brought in earlier that evening. As the door was closed to the outside world, a horse stomped its hooves upon the grass above the side of the building, shook out its mane and galloped away with a loud snort, the dark cape of its rider floating behind in the wind. He had seen all he needed to see.

Inside the meat was divided and devoured, the ale poured and drunk. Elizabeth Device sat in her mother's now vacant rocking chair barking orders at her son, who spent the biggest part the evening filling up tankards and replenishing plates. The room was filled with a gaggle of chatter.

"Any news on th' business wi' yer muvver? said a croaked voice from the hearth.

Elizabeth whistled through her teeth.

"Nah" she answered sharply. "Not that they'd tell me owt in any case".

"Have they got a case 'gainst her tho? the crone continued, " can owt be proved?"

The question made James stop dead in the middle of the floor, the ale continuing to flow unchecked from the partially tipped jug until the targeted vessel overflowed to the floor. Elizabeth stared into the flickering fire and said nothing. Suddenly every other conversation had stopped, enveloping the room in an eerie hush.

"Like to see 'em try" piped up another voice from the shadows.

"How can they prove th' use of magic?"

"Ne'er mind that" said another, younger voice. "They'll find a way sure enuff, if they're mind to it"

A low murmur of agreement spread through the group.

"If only we could do summat"

Suddenly there was a loud crack, the whole house rattled under its power. The flames fanned in the grate for a moment as a freezing gust of wind blew through the building. Large raindrops begin to bounce on the roof as the thunder unleashed for a second, third, fourth time.

"Such as what?" Elizabeth finally spoke, rising from her chair, " what wud ye have us do? Break 'em free? Blow th' castle to smithereens, what?"

With that she stalked from the room and slammed the door, leaving her guests to whisper among themselves as to the possible truth of the rumours surrounding Malkin Tower. James considered following his mother but, deeming it prudent to remain where he was, continued to play host. Up on the top step of the worm eaten staircase, little Jennet Device heard the words, committed them to memory, rose and crept silently to bed.

Roger Nowell was still in his study when the sound of hooves reached his ears from the partially open window. He didn't wait for the man to reach the front door, nor for a servant to allow him entry, but himself went to greet his visitor. The man removed his now dripping cape and hat and hung them on the brass coat stand in the hall, kicked off his boots and followed the magistrate into the study. Nowell ushered him into a chair and carefully closed the door.

" Well?" He enquired, holding out a glass of brown shimmering liquid to the shivering man.

"I assume, since you're here, that you have something to report?"

"Yes, sir" the man took a gulp of the whiskey. " they're having a meet as we speak!"

Nowell turned to face the man, a strange glint in his usually pale eyes.

"A meet? What manner of meet?"

"Well, I'm not entirely sure, not being in the house with them sir. But there is some kind of gathering happening"

"You are sure?" Nowell was leaving nothing to chance. He had to be certain the information would be secure in a trial.

"Saw them arriving for myself sir" the man ran his hand through his damp dark hair and drained his glass.

"Thirteen of them entered that abominable place, then the Demdike daughter closed the door shut behind them. That was when I turned heel and came straight here to you".

Nowell patted the man on the shoulder.

"You did well" he said, handing him a small velvet bag with gold threaded drawstrings.

His guest took the offering and peered inside.

"It's all there" Nowell added, "exactly as was agreed". The man pulled the strings closed and indicated his satisfaction with a nod.

"Can't be too careful sir" he said, rising from his chair and placing the glass down on the table beside him. Nowell looked into his face, a sly smile spreading slowly over his own.

"Indeed, good man, indeed" he replied, holding out a hand. " However, I can assure you that I always honour an agreement"

"Pleased to hear it, Mr Nowell" the man smiled, accepting the handshake while keeping his gaze fixed firmly on his companion. With a second nod he left the room, collecting his belongings and striding out into the stormy night. Within minutes he and his horse had galloped out of sight.

Back in his study, Nowell began to pace the floor, his ears ringing with the information he had just be given. A meeting up at Malkin Tower – he had been waiting for this chance for weeks and now it had dropped into his lap like a gift from the gods. But what was he to do with it? Part of him wanted to ride up there and arrest the whole congregation immediately but one glance out into the night told him that that was not a good idea. The darkness without was suddenly illuminated by a giant flash, followed not too distantly by a rumble so loud that it appeared the whole earth was shaking beneath him. Drops almost the size of golf balls fell and splattered on the ground, collecting together to form ever increasing pools of water that rippled outwards across the gravel. To go out into that, at that time of night, would be a step too far, especially for a gentleman. No, the business up at Malkin would have to wait.

19

There was a strange wailing sound coming from somewhere in the room. Alison rubbed her eyes and peered into the darkness, wondering what on earth could be making such an ominous noise. It was of no use; the room was blacker than a starless Winter midnight, and it hurt her eyes trying to focus on anything beyond her own hand, although that too was slowly turning the same, deep shade of black as the hours, the days, passed silently by. Something scurried over her feet, her skin tingling at the touch as the rest of her body recoiled in both horror and fear. She wasn't scared of the dark so much as what may be lurking within it. She had no idea what else was confined in that cramped dungeon, with its damp, cold stone walls and floor, and its revolting odour of faeces and heaven only knows what else. The something bit the top of her toe. She let out a high pitched yelp and kicked out, forgetting that her leg was chained to the ring in the centre of the room. The iron dug into her skin, and she once more yelled out with the pain. Something shuffled at the other side of the room as a familiar voice barked through the abyss.

– it made little difference to her. She determined that she would answer nothing more about it.

Nowell refused to take the hint and pressed on with his inquiries.

"Mrs Whittle, was the reported land dispute connected with this...how shall we put it… disagreement between Nutter and your daughter?"

Now that the question had moved - albeit not far - from directly concerning her Annie's honour Chattox was more inclined to answer Nowell's question, particularly as the shadow could now be cast over the illustrious name of Nutter rather than that of herself. Tapping the tip of her finger on the top of her stick, she replied.

"Aye sir, indeed it did, for Misser Nutter didn't take kindly to being cast off sir. Left in a proper temper he did, and made all kinds of threats.

He thret' that she would ne'er dwell upon the land should it ever fall into his hands sir. Ye see, our small house lies upon Gawthorpe lands sir"

"Of that I am aware" Nowell said, remembering all the information he already possessed.

"He threatened to turn you off the land, should the chance ever arise"

"Aye sir".

"Stop yer whinin' an yelpin' girl. There ain't no need for it, nor no remedy'll fix it, so be hushed will ye"

"Someat took a bit o' me foot", Alison replied, her voice beginning to shake.

"I'll be bitin' the both of ye, if ye don't stop tha' mitherin'" another voice resonated from the corner.

Alison felt the tears pricking her eyes. She knew it was pointless to argue with her Grandmother – many a clout around the ears had boxed any such notion clear out of her head – so she quietly leaned her head back against the wall and closed her eyes, hoping that when she opened them again she would see something different. It didn't work; all was as it was only seconds earlier. She wished her mother was there. In truth, she wished *she* was with her mother – out there on the big hill, rather than inside this dingy little hole that was so far beneath the ground that no light ever penetrated its walls, making it impossible to discern night from day. She didn't want her mother in there, despite their sometimes fractious relationship. She wouldn't wish for a rat to be in there, and fortune knows she hated them with all of her being. Raising her head, she stared at the ceiling – or what she believed must be the ceiling -, sighed deeply and allowed the tears to fall.

Suddenly there was a loud scraping noise from somewhere above her head, followed by a second, louder creaking and the sound of boots on the stone staircase. Alison turned turned her head in the opposite direction. No visitor down there in the previous weeks have been either welcome or comforting. This was one was likely no exception.

"Elizabeth Southern".

The voice boomed through the space, bouncing off the stone like cannon fire. Nobody spoke. The voice came again.

"Elizabeth Southern"

Alison turned her head in the opposite direction. There had been very few visitors here in the previous week, and those that had ventured into the depths had brought nothing pleasant. She guessed that this one would be no different. Still there was no reply to the call. No sound, save for the scurrying of the something at the far side of the room. A third, much louder attempt was issued.

"Elizabeth Southern. Identify yourself!"

Somebody shifted. There came a croaking growl from within the darkness.

"I heard ye. No need fer shoutin'"

"Get up and come forth"

"Nay sir, I be but an old woman. And I be kept in these 'stances like a rat in a sewer. For nuttin' I might add. Nay Sir. Ye want to talk wi' me, happen you'd better come 'ere instead!"

Alison half smiled to herself. Even now, even here, her grandmother could still make commands. There was no one who would mess with old Demdike. The voice seemed less impressed. It manoeuvred its boots down the stairs and into the dungeon, standing on the tail of one of the resident rodents and cursing the creature beneath its breath, as though it had purposefully got in its way. A light flickered to her right; a dull light that seemed to dance as though suspended in mid air, throwing out the possibility of ominous, unseen shadows. It floated closer, until she could smell the burning candle directly above her head. Raising her head, Alison could just make out the sight of a face looming in the space. She recognised it as that of Mr Covell, warden of the castle and the man responsible for her current care. He leaned in to take a closer look at the dirt covered wretch before him; all four prisoners looked the same to him in the absence of daylight. To him, they weren't women at all. They were animals. Worse than that – they were witches!

Seconds later he turned, seemingly satisfied that Alison was not the person he was searching for, and continued the search, his boots squelching on the grime covered floor as he located his prey, rousing her with a quick, hard kick to the leg. The old woman yelped. Alison closed her eyes in a combination of fear and relief. Fear of what Covell wanted with her elderly grandmother, and of what may happen in the days to come. Relief that, at least for the time being, it was not her that was the target.

Old Demdike was hauled unceremoniously to her feet, every movement eliciting a deep groan as her bones creaked with age and activity.

"What are ye' wantin' fer now?" She snapped. "Can ye not just leave an old woman be'?".

"If it were up to me" Covell snapped, "left is just what you would be. Left, here, to rot. The whole rotten pack of you, and make no mistake. But it isn't up to me – the magistrate wishes to see you, and see you he shall! Though I am wondering that he hasn't seen quite enough of your like already."

With that, he made another grab at her arm and pushed her rudely towards the door.

"I tell you, I will be more than glad to see the backs of you dirty lot, that's one thing for sure!".

The old woman swung her head round in one sudden movement, unleashing a hail of spit into the face of her captor. Alison couldn't see the offence, but she could hear it, and knew precisely what her grandmother had done. She winced and coiled further into the shadows. Covell wiped his face with the arm of his sleeve and proceeded to march towards the exit.

"Perhaps you will *never* be rid of me", Alison heard her hiss before the door slammed shut once more. An uncomfortable silence descended in the room. No one spoke. It was almost as though no one dared breathe.

Demdike was dragged up the staircase and into the main body of the tower, her eyes blinking quickly as they saw light for the first time in days. People were milling around, going about their business as though everything was normal. Nobody stopped to look at the bedraggled old woman who was suddenly among them; even those who took a moment to acknowledge Covell paid no heed to his companion. It was as though her time below ground had rendered her invisible. Not altogether so, for the warden could clearly see her as he manoeuvred her roughly across the stone floor, through an exit at the far side, and into the magistrate's room. At least that's what she assumed it was. There had been a sign, but they had been moving too fast for her to see it properly, not that it would have made any difference if she had – she would not have been able to decipher the words.

Once in the room, Covell flung her onto a seat, brushed off his hands and shirt with a disdainful look on his face and retreated to the door. Demdike heard him bark a precise "watch her!" to someone outside the room before stalking into the distance, boots clattering as he departed. Demdike closed her eyes and shuffled down into her seat. Her sleep had been interrupted by her hasty removal, she was bored and weary, and there was no telling how long she would be waiting. She may as well get comfortable while she can. The next thing she knew she was being moved again, this time into a standing position, by two strong arms that pulled her from either side and set her on her feet in a less than gracious manner. She shook off their grasp and straightened herself as much as her stooped spine would allow.

"Elizabeth Southern?"

She was beginning to tire of the sound of her own name.

"Who wants to know?" she responded sulkily.

"Nicholas Bannister, Magistrate!"

Demdike grunted, but offered nothing more.

"Shall I assume that that is whom you are?".

Again, he received no reply.

Bannister sighed deeply, picked up his quill and quickly scribbled something onto the paper in front of him before handing it to the waiting clerk, who then left the room. The guards at her side retreated backwards as the magistrate stepped out from behind the desk and moved towards her. She didn't flinch, nor did she look away, instead maintaining a steely glare in his direction. He was not discouraged. He stopped within touching distance of the old woman and lowered himself almost to her height so as to look her directly in the eye. They stood, staring at each other in this way, for what seemed an age before either of them made to break the silence. In the end, it was he that did so.

"Mrs Southern". He spoke sharply, as though already irritated by the conversation.

"The magistrate in Pendle has requested that I meet with you, to check some new information that has come to light".

"What *information?*" she half spat out the second word as though the possibility meant nothing to her.

"I have answered all yer questions already!"

"Ah, but today is not about questions." Bannister smiled. "At least, not to begin with".

Demdike was confused. If there were no questions, why had she been brought here, paraded like cattle through the castle. Bannister watched her with suspicion.

"We have heard tell that you, Mrs Southern, are well practised in the dark arts, and that you have the very mark of the devil branded upon your skin".

There was no reaction from the old woman. Her wizened face betrayed no emotion whatsoever, yet internally she was frantically trying to comprehend his words. She was aware of the idea of the Devil's Mark, but had never actually seen one. She had no idea what one would even look like; nor how one would even *get* such a thing. If they even existed, which she doubted they did. Either way she was certain that she did not possess anything of the sort. Bannister took her silence as insolence and called forth the guards, one of whom he issued with a folded piece of paper and the instruction to locate Mr Nowell. The guard nodded and departed on his quest.

For a while nobody spoke. The old woman and the magistrate stared at each other, as though one were attempting to break the other with pure silence, a game at which neither party appeared willing to be defeated. At length the door opened to admit the familiar face of Roger Nowell, and the guard charged with his deliverance. Nowell cast a disdainful look in Demdike's direction before engaging Bannister in whispered conversation, their backs turned on the woman who formed the subject of their debate. She was left to stand, staring into mid air, for what felt like half a lifetime.

"Mrs Southern".

The voice startled her back into the room. The men were facing her now, their discussion seemingly ended.

"Mrs Southern, we feel we must perform an examination – to determine the presence, or otherwise, of any such mark upon you."

 A strange shiver ran down the length of her spine; at once her nostrils flared and her breathing became both slower and deeper than it had previously been. The two guards stepped forwards; she could feel their presence at her shoulders like they were the devil himself. Suddenly there was a jerking motion as her gown was pulled swiftly downwards, revealing her naked frame to the room. Instinctively the elderly woman threw her arms across herself; rough hands prevented them from reaching their destination, holding them firmly out at angle from which she could not pull free. Pain shot through her body as she waited for the magistrates to begin their examination, which they did with little consideration for their aged subject. Seconds passed into minutes; minutes that felt like hours. She could feel their eyes on her skin, their hands touching her every so often as they scoured every single patch of her past eighty years old body. Only one man had ever seen her naked in the whole of her life. She thought of him now – her long gone husband, her Thomas, the man who had taken her as his wife with disregard to her scandalous past. The man who had chosen to accept and raise her illegitimate child as his own rather than lose the girl he loved. Hot tears burned her eyes, she struggled to keep them from escaping down her cheeks. She would *not* allow these men, these rude, uncivilised jailers to see her cry. She, Elizabeth Southern, once an Ingham wife, once a daughter of the Blackburn family of Whalley, had never suffered such humiliation, even when cast into the depths of poverty with the death of her beloved Thomas. She may have nothing else, but she still had some pride. They could not, they *would* not be allowed to take that from her too.

"Heaven save us" a voice declared, bringing her back to the situation at hand. Nowell had stepped backwards, his spectacles in his right hand, his face contorted into an almost panicked grimace. Bannister and the guards followed suit, allowing Demdike the freedom of her arms once more. Slowly she lowered the aching limbs back to the sides of her body, her eyes never moving from the large wooden cross that sat on the wall opposite. She knew immediately that the outcome was unfavourable.

The two magistrates huddled before the desk, their backs turned to her as they quickly debated their discovery. Demdike's gown was pulled back upwards; she clasped it around herself in grateful modesty while waiting for her fate to be decided. Nobody spoke aloud. Nobody looked at anybody else. The room suddenly became heavy with anticipation.

"Mrs Southern" Bannister began, his face suddenly a much paler shade of white. "Are you aware that you carry the mark of the devil himself upon your skin?"

Demdike shifted on her feet. Bannister continued. Nowell scribbled furiously on a piece of paper.

"On your left side, you possess a blue mark, almost the size of the back of my thumb. Please, explain to us how this came to be".

Demdike hesitated. She knew no explanation would satisify their question, save for the one they were hoping would be forthcoming.

"It's a mark of birth Sir, nothing more" she replied calmly.

"A birth mark?" Nowell repeated.

"And how did this 'birth mark' come to be upon you? Was your mother a witch, Mrs Southern? Did she train you in the dark arts herself?. Perhaps she sold your soul to the devil, and he left his claim upon you there? What say you to that?"

"I was born wi' it, and shall no doubt die wi' it Sir. My mother was no witch, nor my father, nor any of my kin. They were God fearin' folks so they were, and would think no more o' curses and spells than ye would o' dancin' a naked int' streets o' Pendle. I know not the origins of birth marks, nor how they come to appear, but I tell ye this; no divil, nor it's familiars left that mark upon me, as God himsel' be my witness"

Nowell and Bannister exchanged glances. At that moment, Demdike knew.

20

Ashlar House stood in solitary confinement on the Fence road, shielded by a small dip in the ground behind which the foundations had been built some centuries earlier. It's remote position left it open to the wild, temperamental elements of the Lancashire countryside weather, therefore it had been constructed of the finest bricks and materials available in order to withstand whatever came its way. The rear opened onto a vast, sweeping landscape of green fields that stretched for as far as the eye could see, interspersed with the occasional cluster of trees or bushes in the distance, and the tiniest specks of farms and dwellings that resided well into the distance. It was here that Roger Nowell and Nicholas Bannister arrived on a cold morning at the end of April to continue their pursuit of witches working in the shadow of the hill.

They were joined on this occasion by a third man, a Mr Thomas Potts, who had been employed for services of scribing the meeting that was to happen on that morning. The two magistrates had come to the decision that everything from this point should be preserved in written form, by someone other than themselves for the purposes of a possible trial, particularly as that appeared to be becoming a much more obvious conclusion with every passing day. Nowell had also insisted that a written document, sent personally to the King himself, would earn him – would earn *both* of them – a great deal of personal praise and favour that could only be favourable to them in the future. Bannister had considered this point, and hired Potts for the job.

And so it was that, just before the chime of midday, James Device was ushered into the large hall and given a seat before the three distinguished and severe looking officials. He immediately settled down into the luxury of the chair, having never been offered one at any other of the meetings he had been brought to, and surveyed the room. This was clearly the home of a man of wealth, for the walls were adorned with rich tapestries and fine paintings. James wondered what manner of man the owner was, and how he had come to own a house such as this. He surely knew nobody with such means. He stared for a moment at the man in the corner, bent over a table with his quill poised. Was this man writing about him? He wondered. Was he about to become useful at last? Roger Nowell cleared his throat with a loud cough and shuffled some papers on the desk in front of him. Bannister donned his spectacles, nodded to the scribe, and the session began.

There followed a flurry of questions regarding the events of the Good Friday just passed, and the meeting that had taken place at Malkin Tower. James admitted that he had caught and stolen a sheep from the field of John Robinson at Barley, and that he had carried it home as food for the guests expected that same afternoon. When asked if he knew the names of the guests he hesitated, unsure as to whether he should be giving that information or not. Nowell stroked his beard and looked at the wretched child before him. He knew exactly how to glean the required information.

"James, do you want to help the King?" he asked.

James sat upright in his seat. The King was far away in London. What had any of this to do with the King? What did the King care about the goings on of the poor folks up in the wilds of Lancashire?

"Our business here touches the King himself greatly" Nowell continued, seizing the boy's new interest in the matter at hand. "It's conclusion is of personal interest to His Majesty, and he is kept informed at all stages".

Nowell looked at Bannister from the corner of his eye. Bannister recognised his partner's plan instantly and returned the gesture. This was how to make the boy talk.

"Don't you see, James?" Bannister took over, "you helping us today could be of tremendous help to the King"

"Help that His Majesty would be extremely...grateful for".

Again, the two men cast a glance at one another over the rims of their spectacles. James heard the words swimming around inside his head. He, James Device, of Malkin Tower, and of no use to anyone, ever, could actually help the King himself? Could that even be possible? He decided that he was not going to waste the possibility, even if it came to naught. Nowell and Bannister had caught the boy in their well laid trap.

"Tell us James, who *were* the people at Malkin Tower on Good Friday?"

He thought for a moment. Nothing of note had happened on that day. Nobody had done anything wrong. What harm could come from these men knowing their names?

"I don't know all of them" he said. "Some I ain't never seen not spoke to afore that day".

"That's ok" Nowell soothed. "Just give us the names you know for now".

"Well" he said slowly, trying to recall. "There were my uncle, Christopher Holgate. He were there, wi' his wife. Pretty gal she is. Dunno why she be wi' him so I don't"

"Your uncle is a Holgate?" Bannister asked in mock surprise. James was taken aback; surely this man knew about that. *Everyone* knew about that.

"Erm, yes Sir. An 'olgate he is by birth. We ain't never bin too sure as to who 'is favver were, but he were a 'olgate fer sure. My grandmother names 'im so, so his pa must a bin a 'olgate. Do ye see?"

Bannister did see. Of course he was well aware of Elizabeth Southern's illegitimate son. It was no secret in these parts, nor had it ever been. For low down folks such as her, these things were considered unimportant, expected even. Neither were they important now, save for the fact that the son was now implicated in the events of the Good Friday meet.

"Who else?" he coaxed gently.

James thought for a moment, counting silently on his fingers.

"There were the wife of Hugh Hargreaves, o'er Burnley way. Dunno her name though.

And Jane and John Bulcock, of them as owns Black Moss Farm. Old man Bulcock weren't there though. Just the wife and son."

Potts scribbled furiously as the names came tumbling from the boy's mouth.

"Let's see. There be the wife of Christopher Hargreaves of Thorneyholme, and Alice Grey from Colne. There was erm….Katherine Hewitt, old Mouldheel's wife, and…."

James stopped as he desperately tried to remember the other name. He could picture the woman in his head, but the name escaped him. All three men simultaneously looked up from their papers in anticipation.

"Nutter!" he exclaimed, triumphant at having remembered at last. "Alice Nutter of Roughlee. She were t'other one that were there".

A strange half smile spread across Nowell's face. He was more than aware of the Nutter family at Roughlee; they had proved a thorn in his side, and pocket, on more than one occasion. This could be just what he was looking for.

"Oh and my ma of course, and me. And our Jennet, but she were upstairs the 'ole time. She weren't any part of th'meetin' cos she's only a babby".

"Of course, of course" Bannister said, waving a hand. "So that is eleven so far, not including the child upstairs. Any more to add, young James?"

"No Sir. There were others there, but I dunno the names, as I said afore."

"Well, that's very helpful James" Nowell said, sitting forwards in his seat. "Now, it would be even *more* useful to know exactly what the meeting was about. The King would be most interested in that!"

"To talk about me sister and grandmother, and them bein' tekken away in that cart."

"What about them?"

"Well, whether we could do owt about it".

"And was anything suggested, at the meeting?"

"Only that we could blow up the castle and let em out. Nuffin else. Was a waste of time if ye ask me!".

Both men sat back in their seats, very much interested in this suggestion, unable to decipher whether or not it had been said in a manner of sarcasm or seriousness. Either way, it could not be tolerated.

"The King is very serious in his study of magic and witchcraft, James. Was there anything of that nature talked about on that day?"

James desperately wanted to be of help to the King.

"Well" he began. "There was talk of Alison's dog, although I didn't understand this cos she ain't got no dog, nor is ever like to have one at Malkin. Grandmother ain't too keen on dogs ye see, says they make too much noise, leave too much mess, and cost too much money. And we ain't got none o' that."

"And how did the meet finish?"

"Well, they all left the house together, except for ma and me, of course, although we went outside to bid 'em farewell and see 'em off. And there were horses awaitin' 'em, though I dunno where from cos most of 'em didn't have horses to their names. The horses were small, and some were brown in colour, and others were as black as night. Except Jennet Preston. She had brought her white foal wi' her. The colour of smooth snow it were. So white and shiny. And then they went and vanished over th' hill, like into nowtness. Just disappeared".

"Tell me, James, have you ever had any dealings with dark magic?"

James grinned as he thought of the story he was about to tell. This should make his name once and for all, he thought. The King would study him and his family to learn about witchcraft, and they would be known as helpers of the Court. They would have something to be proud of at last. He chewed on his bottom lip as he finalised the details in his head.

"Well..." he began, "about two years ago, just afore Easter, my grandmother sent me to church to take communion. She told me I had not to eat the bread, but to hide it on meself, and give it to 'a Thing' that I would meet on't way 'ome. Well, I dint know what she were meanin' but off I went and took the communion at New Church. But I ate the bread, even though she bade me not to, cos I were hungry, and I dint know what she were on about. So I ate it and set off for 'ome. About two hundred yards or so from th' church there appeared a thing that looked like a hare, but were not a hare. It asked me for the bread that had been blessed at th' church, but I couldn't give it to 'im cos i'd eaten it already. The hare thing was not best happy, and told me it'd have the devil himsel' upon me for not givin' him th' bread. I was afeared, I was, and dint know what to do, so I crossed meself, marked meself to God I did, and the Thing just vanished afore me. Gone, just like that!"

"And then, on the following Easter, I met my Dandy, who came to me as a black dog with a long tail and bushy fur, and teeth as big an' sharp as I ever did see. I told him my soul belonged to Saviour Jesus Christ, but that I would right give 'im the rest of me if he wanted it. He bit me on th' arm and then went away."

James was enjoying his stories now. He told himself that nobody was going to believe any of it, and if it was of use to the King and these fine gentlemen, then there could be no trouble to come from it. A little bit of fantasy was harmless surely, he thought.

"That's very interesting" Bannister replied, when the boy stopped to take a breath.

"Now James, what can you tell us about Alice Nutter?"

"She comes from a good family does Mrs Nutter. They live over Roughlee way I think. Somewhere near Crowtrees."

"And what does she have to do with all this business?"

"Ummm, well, I dunno if I should say Sir. Cos I can't say as to whether it be truth or not Sir!"

"You tell us what you can, we will determine the truth of it" Nowell rejoined.

"Ummm, well, my grandmother told me that the three of 'em – herself, Mrs Nutter and my ma, had dealt with someone at Roughlee cos of an argument. That they had tekken 'im out, though I dunno how they done it. Perhaps it were the figures, but I dunno."

"Figures?", Nowell leaned forwards once more. He needed to hear more of this.

"Aye Sir. Figures. Made of clay and dried afore a fire. If ye make em with a particular likeness, then crumble them, it's said that the person who's likeness they are will die soon enough".

"And this person at Roughlee. He died?"

"Aye Sir, Henry Mitton it were. He wouldn' give my grandmother a penny when she asked 'im. Next thing, he were dead and gone, and for no reason they could find."

Nowell pressed him more on the clay figures. Here, surely, was the evidence he needed.

James was more than happy to oblige. He gave them a story about three such images being seen at the home of Anne Redfern and her family about two years previously. He said that each of the Redfern family had been holding one, while he watched from behind a hedgerow. Anne Redfern's image had crumbled in her hands, but he couldn't say whose likeness it had been. From there, he told how Chattox had taken three skulls from the New Church graveyard and removed eight of the teeth, half of which she had given to Demdike on the following day. To give credence to his story, he explained how he had found the teeth buried at the west end of Malkin Tower, alongside a crumbled image of the daughter of Anthony Nutter. Nowell and Bannister listened with incredulity to the boy's words. If any of this were true, they now had enough to send all the named parties to trial.

James was thanked for his time and his information and dismissed from the room, accompanied by a guard who would keep him company until he was next required. Happy in the belief that he had been of some use at last, and that the King himself may find favour with him, the boy took his leave.

21

Next it was his mother's turn to answer the questions.

Elizabeth Device stood in the middle of the room, her lazy eye wandering in one direction while its more constant counterpart remained fixed firmly on the wall straight ahead of her, her hands clenched tightly around the waistline of her faded grey gown. She took little notice of the two magistrates who awaited her, nor of Mr Potts seated a little way to her right. They were of little importance to her; she had been here before. It was Bannister who began the enquiry.

"Mrs Device" he said slowly, "we meet again!"

Elizabeth breathed deeply.

"Aye Sir" she muttered. "I wish I could say it were a pleasure!"

Bannister's top lip curled upwards as he studied this curious woman. She had no beauty to speak of, and such a lack of education and propriety that would make any mother embarrassed to be associated with, and yet she had the gall, the audacity to speak to a man such as himself in such tones. Very rude, he thought to himself. Very unladylike behaviour. But then, she was a creature of the hills, a possible daughter of the Devil himself. Perhaps he should not be too surprised. Besides, there were more important matters at hand. He pressed on.

"Tell us about Good Friday".

"Good Friday?" she rejoined, "You mean, the day on which our Lord was put to death on th' Cross and the rose again? Aye Sir, I'd a' thought a man like you would have had th' learnin' o' that in yer posh eddication, so I would".

Bannister cast her a death like stare from across the table. He could feel his face growing steadily warmer with anger. He must not let this woman get to him, not at any cost.

"Mrs Device, I am more than well aware of the meaning behind Good Friday, and I am more than convinced that you know that that is not what I meant. This is no time for games, Mrs Device. Tell us what happened at your home on the Good Friday just passed, if you please".

"Well, why did you not ask that the first time?" she said, revelling somewhat in the magistrate's clear discomfort. "Now, let me see. Good Friday."

She paused, pretending to think about her answer. Nowell shifted in his seat. Bannister grew increasingly more frustrated.

"Oh yes, I remember. Our Jam bringed us a sheep back, so he did. Got it from somewher' o'er Barley way I think. I dunno. Anyways, we had some folks o'er and had a meal like we ain't had fer some time, I tell ye."

"These folks" Bannister interjected, wincing at his use of the vernacular. "I mean, these *people.* Would they be the people on this list?"

He read back the names that James had given them less than an hour previously. Elizabeth nodded with each name announced.

"Aye Sir, that'd be them. Fine folks they be an' all".

"I'm sure" said Nowell, "Mrs Device, are you aware that these people are all on a list of possible witches in the area?"

"I had heard so, although from what I hear that most o' th' folks around th' hill are on such a list. Indeed, all us simple folks must be witches, we must needs be practisin' magic to survive where I be from and no mistake."

Nowell and Bannister both looked down at their papers. Neither dared to glance sideways at their partner. Was this the confession they were hoping for?

"How do you mean?" came a small voice from the corner. Elizabeth turned her head slowly to look at the speaker. Mr Potts suddenly remembered his place and looked apologetically at the other two men before returning his gaze to the task he had been employed to perform.

"I mean, Sir, that there must be some divine – or dark – force at work on th' hill for all us folks to go on livin', so there must. We ain't got no money, nor are there hopes of any 'ployment for th' likes of us. Begging be all we be good fer, and that ain't putting food on th' table reight. How any of us go on survivin' up there is some kind a' magic in itsel' Sir. That's what I meant".

Potts didn't raise his head. Bannister and Nowell continued their questions.

"Did you talk of your daughter and mother, and their current situation, at this gathering?"

"It came up Sir, as it were bound to do, them not bein' at th' house as they should a been."

"And was there talk of blowing up the castle?"

Elizabeth was stunned for a moment. She recalled saying something like that in the heat of the moment. although the actual words had long since left her memory. The question in her mind was how that one comment had reached the ears of these two men so far away from both Malkin Tower and Pendle Hill itself. She smelled a snitch, and she could possibly guess at who.

"Mrs Device". The sound of her name brought her back into the present with a start. "Please answer the question!"

"Blowin' up th' castle Sir. That's brave talk and no mistake. How would such as I go about doin' a thing like that? Can barely afford to blow me own nose. No Sir, I dont remember owt like that bein' talked of, not at all".

"Who were the other people present?. We know there were more there in your house than the names we have here. We need names, Mrs Device".

"One were Anne Cronkshaw" she shrugged, "from over Marsden way. Two of t' others were folks that old Mrs Nutter knew. From th' Burnley parish I think".

Nowell noted the names onto the bottom of the list.

"What are your relations with a Mr John Robinson of Barley?"

Elizabeth snorted.

"Relations?" she spat. "Why I have no relations with that man, nor would I ever have th' mind to do so."

"Died suddenly didn't he, Mr Robinson?"

"Aye Sir. That he did. A good few years back though. Can't say as I were sorry to see him go. He made no small 'mount of trouble for me when I had my Jennet, so he did. Told everyone who'd hear that i'd had a bebby outta marriage. Told 'em I were an 'ore and that my bebby were a spawn o' vice. Of course most people were a listnin' to him, cos he had a loud voice and knew lots of folks, so he did. The folks that gave me money for jobs, or for beggin' stopped giving ye see. And me with a small 'un to feed, as well as me ma and th' other two I have. No, made things very 'ard for me did John Robinson. I could a' killed him for how he tret me, I could."

"And did you?"

Elizabeth looked at Nowell for the first time that day. They exchanged stares for a few moments, neither speaking a word.

"No Sir, I did not."

"So, you did not make an image of him in clay and destroy it, thereby killing him from afar?"

Silence once more filled the room. Elizabeth looked at the magistrate, wondering whether he had finally lost his mind. Nowell watched her carefully, ready to pounce.

"Sir, I thought ye were a eddicated man, not a man who readily believes in such nonsense as that. Why, if that were possible there would be a good many bodies found, of that I can assure ye. I 'ave heard talk of such things I admit, but I never thought it was real. Most folks don't Sir. Its stuff and nonsense. Fairy talk. I don't be believin' in it, and neither should you Sir. Why, If a man could be killed in such a way, I'd a done ye in when ye took my child from me, and my ma. Don't ya think I'd a done that Sir?"

Nowell shuddered at the very suggestion. For the first time since beginning this quest, he felt rather frightened of the little woman he had called before him. Not too long later, Elizabeth Device was dismissed from the room. Once alone, the two men sunk into their seats, their minds buzzing with information, ideas and notions of dark happenings on the old, silent hillside. There was no doubt about it, these people had to be stopped.

22

The enquiry at Ashlar House had left the two magistrates with a great deal to think about. The net had suddenly been cast much wider than either of them had ever anticipated and, armed with the list of new names, they came up with a new plan of investigation. They would speak to each of these new people and learn their secrets. There appeared to be a lot of rivalry and tension on the hill; with any luck, these people would soon turn on each other and tongues would loosen. If they could prove the existence of witchcraft, and exterminate it, the names of Roger Nowell and Nicholas Bannister would be written in history; witch finders and faithful servants of the great King James. They could become famous. They had work to do.

The first task was to bring in the hitherto unnoticed witness that had just been brought to their attention, and to see what they could add to the narrative. And so it was that nine year old Jennet Device found herself at the centre of the investigation.

23

The small, brown haired child peered nervously around the door, unsure as to where she found herself, and what was waiting on the other side. She saw a large room with a desk at the far side and another set a little way off into the corner. She saw the large wooded cross that was set on the far wall, and the images of a robed man with a long beard and a far away look in his downcast eyes. She saw three well dressed gentlemen grouped together in quiet discussion over a piece of paper that one of them held in his hand. Every so often he would point at certain words, which would then begin a new flurry of conversation and gesticulation from his colleagues. It was clearly something very important. Jennet watched for a little while before her guardian, who had been engaged in their own debate in the hallway, knocked on the door and ushered her inside. The discussion stopped immediately. One of the men – the tallest one, with the grey hair and deep red waistcoat, motioned for a chair to be brought, onto which the little girl was helped to climb. The two chairs were pulled out from behind the desk, and a third from somewhere she didn't see, one for the guardian, and the others for the two smart men.

"Comfortable?" Bannister asked, his voice suddenly warm and soothing.

Jennet shuffled her bottom on the seat and nodded. Bannister smiled.

"You are a pretty little thing, arent' you?" he mused, studying her carefully. The child blinked. Nobody had said that to her before. She hated her freckled nose and cheeks, her deep set brown eyes, greasy hair and bony, dirt ridden skin. Yet here was a money-man saying she was pretty. She could not quite believe that such a man as this could think that of her. Even her own mother never had. She looked down at her knees, the blush spreading over her face.

"Tell me child" he continued, "what is your name?"

"Jennet" she whispered. "Jennet Device".

He leaned forwards to better hear her.

"Where do you live, Jennet?"

"Malkin Tower. By th' big 'ill".

"And who do you live with?"

"My ma, my bruvver, my sister, and my gramma".

"Where is your father, child?"

Her eyes flicked upwards to meet his, and quickly returned to her lap as she felt a lump form in the back of her throat. She swallowed hard.

"I dunno Sir" she mumbled. "I never knew me favver. Dunno who he is, or if he be alive o' dead, or where he be."

"Would you have liked to have known him?"

Again, she raised her eyes in surprise at the question.

"Why yes Sir, I would a' liked it" she said.

"But ma won't even tell me 'bout 'im, nor will my gramma. Would a' bin nice I spose."

She hesitated, imagining- not for the first time - the father she had conjured up in her mind. His voice was deep and commanding, but loving and warm. She could hear his laughter in her thoughts. He would have been the master of his home, and his word law; her ma would have treated her a fair bit better then. And James too. They wouldn't have dared be mean to her if he had been there, she knew that. She blinked hard to remove the sting of developing tears. How she missed this man that she had never known.

"I heard there was a party at Malkin Tower recently" Bannister went on. He didn't wish to upset the child further on the paternity issue. He needed much more important information.

"Good Friday, was it?".

"Wasn't really a party Sir. Just some folks as me ma knows came for some food and some talkin'"

"Where did the food come from, Jennet?"

"Me bruvver Jam gone and got it from somewhere. Barley I think he said. Not seen so much food in me house ever I ain't."

"Taste good did it?" the man smiled.

"Dunno Sir. I didn't get none. I were sent up to me room and told I 'ad to stay there. Nice things ain't for th' likes o' me".

Bannister felt a slight pang in his chest that such a small child could have such thoughts, much less been told such things. His children had never gone without, and nor should any child if the means be found. He would see that this young girl would be made comfortable in the future.

"So you were upstairs the whole time? I suppose then, you cant tell me anything about it, if you weren't there".

"Oh I can Sir" she said assertively. "I were upstairs, but I weren't in me room as I were told. I were watchin', listnin' from th' stairtop."

This information grabbed both men's attentions. Nowell, who had been only too happy to allow Bannister to deal with the child, sat forwards in his seat in anticipation of what Jennet could be about to tell them. Suddenly Jennet felt important.

"Can you tell us who was there? Let's start with that".

Jennet looked at Nowell for the first time since sitting down. She didn't like the look of him as much as the other man; he was more stricter looking, and his eyes not quite as kind. She decided she would speak only to Bannister.

"There was 'bout twenty folks there" she said, reverting her gaze back to her preferred questioner. "I know who some of 'em are, but not t'others. Shall I tell ye their names?"

"Yes please, Jennet, if you can".

"I can" she said, puffing out her tiny chest.,

"there were the my uncle Holgate, he were there, as were old Mrs Nutter and Hargreaves of Thorneyholme. He brought his wife wi' 'im too. There were me ma a'course, and Jam were allowed down there in th' middle of it all, and the other woman – her as is wed to Hugh Hargreaves. Dunno her real name though. That's all's of 'em I know Sir, but there was more. Two of 'em were men folk, but rest were women".

"Thank you, Jennet", Bannister placed a gentle hand on hers. "That's most helpful".

Jennet smiled. She liked this man.

"Did they mention anything about your sister?" he added, picking a piece of hair from his waistcoat. "About when she might be coming home?"

Jennet snorted.

"Ma says she'd be a fair kind o' lucky if she ever came home. Gramma too. Says they're in sticky mud and that they might be stoppin' at th' castle for a long time. Its a right mess they gotten into, she says. Nowt we can do 'bout it, short a' blowing up th' castle to get 'em out".

Bannister started at the child's choice of words. He was certain they had been used before.

"Where have you heard that?" he snapped, causing the girl to shrink back in her seat. He knew he had scared her, and reached out for her once more. She allowed him to rest a hand on her knee.

"I heard my ma say it to the folks at the house." she said, fighting back the tears.

"We cant be doing that though, can we? Its just silly talk. I didn't mean nuffin' by it".

"Its okay, Jennet" Bannister soothed, rubbing her skin gently. "I know it was just silly talk. No harm done."

Jennet relaxed. The big man wasn't angry with her.

"Do you think your sister did what they say she did?"

She shrugged.

"She probly cursed th' man if he wouldn't give her th' pins. She did that a lot, if she got cross or upset. Ma docs it too, and Jam, and Gramma. Dunno if that's wha' med th' man poorly though."

Bannister nodded slowly, allowing the child's words to sink in.

"Have they ever cursed you?"

"All the time Sir. They don't like me cos o' me not havin' same favver as 'em. Or cos I was got by accident an me ma not wed."

"Have you ever cursed them?"

"No Sir. I have no power, curses'd do me no good, so why'd I bother?"

"But your mother has power? And your grandmother, and the others?"

"If Alison did what they say, then I reckon she must have summat, mustn't she?".

Bannister said nothing.

"What'll happen to her? To them?" Jennet enquired.

"If tried and found guilty, you won't be seeing them for a very long time" Nowell said starkly. Jennet chewed on her bottom lip.

"You mean, they would go to th' gaol. Like what they are now?"

Nobody spoke. She took their silence as confirmation.

"What'll happen to me?" she whispered, "i ain't got no one else. I'll be all by me'sell".

"We will find you somewhere to go, dear. If needs be. Somewhere nice and warm, with nice people, and nice food. Would you like that?"

Jennet considered the question. She pictured herself in a big brick house, with a man and a woman in clean, bright clothes and a big smile. There would be food, and a bath, and a proper bed to lie in, and no more chores, or beatings, or harsh words of any kind. She breathed in the images. She longed for them to be real. Sure, her own folks would probably suffer being locked away in a cell for a while. Maybe they would be forced to scrub floors, and be hit or screamed at for not doing it well enough. Maybe it was their turn to endure the hardships they had inflicted on her all of her life. And she would be living better, and not thinking of them. It would be as much as they deserved, and no mistake.

"Yes Sir. I would like that very much".

"We need... *I* need you to do something very important for me. Can you do that?"

Jennet nodded.

"I want you to think very carefully about your home, and your family. I want you to think about anything strange, or different about them. About what they have done. Anything...magical, shall we say? Any particular curses, any strange deaths or disappearances, anything you can remember. I want you to tell your new guardians anything that comes to mind, in as much detail as possible. Do you think you can do that for me, Jennet?"

The child frowned and screwed up her nose. She was certain she could think of things that might help this nice man, and if her words were fit to punish her family in some way, so much the better. She would think upon it.

Bannister nodded to the guardian, who gently assisted Jennet from the chair, and led her from the room.

"I hope we shall speak again soon, dear Jennet" Bannister called as they reached the door. Jennet looked at him over her shoulder and smiled, lifted her left hand in a small wave, and left. Nowell, Bannister and Potts watched the door close behind her before the latter joined the magistrates in the centre of the room, taking the seat which the Device child had just vacated. The next few hours were spent rereading Potts' notes on the interviews, deliberating the points raised, and deciding what the next course of action was to be. By the time that dinner was announced, the conclusion had been drawn, analysed and drawn a second time. The time was drawing near.

24

The following day was one of swift, decisive action.

Elizabeth Device and her son had not been allowed to leave Ashlar House following their interrogations, and had been brought back before the magistrates to be informed that they would travel immediately to Lancaster Castle to await further proceedings. They had left by cart in the dark and were now safely incarcerated in the dungeon alongside Alison, Demdike and the others, unsure as to precisely what crime they were believed to have committed, or how long they were likely to remain there.

That same cart was now making it's way around the farm houses and other dwellings in Pendle. It had already stopped at Black Moss Farm and collected John and Jane Bulcock, who had been bundled into the rear and fastened to the seat with lengths of hard, uncomfortable rope. It had then called at Barley and picked up the wife of Hugh Hargreaves, and lastly Christopher Holgate and his wife Elizabeth, who were most put out at being removed from their home in such a manner, and made no mistake at their opinions being heard. Their protestations fell on deaf ears, and they were taken on their way.

A short time later, a second cart pulled up to a stop outside the dilapidated home of Katherine Hewitt on the outskirts of Colne, and then at the dwelling of Alice Grey. Both women were told simply by the driver's companion that they must get into the vehicle straight away and not make a fuss. Neither being the kind of woman who would draw any attention to themselves if they could prevent doing so, they followed their orders and were spirited away to Lancaster as fast as the horses could move.

A third cart had been sent to Roughlee to collect old Alice Nutter who, being of decidedly better status than the others, was deemed worthy of solitary transportation.

By nightfall, the dungeon of the castle on the hill held a total of twenty one prisoners, each suspected of witchcraft yet none as yet charged with any crime. Roger Nowell spent the evening writing a long letter to the King's advisers in London, informing them of the happenings in Lancashire, and assuring the reader of his continued determination to root out all malevolent forces in his jurisdiction. That done, he retired to his bed and slept soundly through the remainder of the night.

25

A messenger from the Court arrived in Pendle less than a week later. Nowell read the missive carefully, and pressed it neatly into the cover of his Bible with a barely suppressed smile. The King's advisers had considered his information and decided, upon brief consultation, the allow the local authorities to continue leading the case at hand. No request for a preview of the evidence would be sought, and no requirement to wait for permission to continue. He could proceed at will. There would be no interference from the Court in what was now deemed, officially, to be a Lancashire case. The response had been exactly what he had hoped for.

With that information planted firmly in his mind, Roger Nowell set about his mission with a renewed sense of righteousness and vigour. The paperwork was checked, rechecked, verified and examined a fourth time, with corrections and alterations made at intervals where ever he deemed it necessary to do so in order to make it read more coherently, and salaciously, than it already did. No one would ever know, he told himself; by the time the King's advisors requested the documents – if they ever did – the accused would have been dealt with, and there would be nobody left to contradict his version. The *official* version. After all his hard work, he had to make the charges both convincing and condemning in equal measure. These people had to hang. He could not afford any mistakes.

26

The seventeenth day of May arrived in a hail of Spring rains that lashed the Lancashire countryside like a possessed father punishing his ill behaved offspring. Pools formed on the paths and roads, trees swayed to the rhythm of the wind, some of them too weak to withstand its dance for too long and collapsing to the ground with such force than anything that happened to be in their path suffered a swift and decisive end. It was almost as though some divine judgement was being passed on the people below.

Nowell viewed the scene from the window with a disgruntled expression on his face. It hadn't rained for weeks, yet on the day that he needed to travel a good distance, it was doing so, and with merry abandon. He considered postponing his trip in the hope that the following day would provide more suitable conditions, but then there was little guarantee that tomorrow would be any better. He would just have to endure it.

Calling in his manservant, he ordered his carriage to be prepared immediately, and word to be sent down to the kitchen that he would not be home for dinner that evening – much to the delight of the cook, for it gave her an unexpected night away from the oven, and the half-witted serving girls that went with it. The servant departed with the instructions, and Nowell returned to his desk, took one final look over the sheets of writing that lay there, and placed them carefully into the paper sheath in which he would transport them to their destination. Minutes later the horses arrived outside the entrance, the metal carriage fastened tightly to their harnesses and shimmering in the translucence of the falling rain. Nowell threw on his cloak and hat, swept up the sheath beneath the material to keep it dry, and set forth.

The roads between Pendle and Lancaster were difficult to pass that day. The winds blew against the carriage, causing it to sway and jolt in all directions, the hard rain pelting the roof with a sound that reminded him of a drum beating somewhere close at hand. The horses slugged and moaned, the driver employed the use of his whip to maintain their progress and Nowell sat upright within, contemplating the day, the weeks, the tasks ahead. He didn't think too much about what was happening outside; the weather was the horses' problem, the conditions and the journey were issues for the driver. It was their job to get him to where he needed to go, not his to worry about the journey.

Lancaster castle loomed large in the distance, its stone gatehouse standing tall against the increasingly darkening sky. Nowell shuddered at the enormity of the giant, silently threatening stonework that rose before him as the carriage pulled to a halt in the courtyard. As he surveyed the edifice, a tall man in a guard's robe appeared, his boots stomping on the damp cobblestones as he approached.

"Excuse me, Sir" he said, his voice firm.

"Please state the purpose for your visit".

Nowell turned. The guard immediately softened his stance and nodded in acknowledgement.

"My apologies, Sir. I did not recognise you for a moment".

"No harm done, Roberts, no harm done" Nowell responded with a smile.

"I trust the others are arrived?"

"Mr Bannister and Mr Wilsey arrived earlier, Sir. They are in the courtroom. The others are still to come."

"Thank you, Roberts" Nowell cocked his head slightly to one side in a sort of bow. Roberts half bowed and marched back to his sentry position at the far side of the yard. Nowell watched him leave, before turning, taking one more look at the view before him and making his way quickly through the entrance, and into the main body of the castle.

He was greeted on route by Covell, who held out a thick hand to the magistrate, who accept it with a firm shake. Nowell looked at the older man's face, the ominous feeling that something was amiss creeping slowly through him.

"What ails you, Covell?" he asked.

The warden looked hard at his feet before answering the question, unsure of how to approach the problem, certain that Nowell was not going to like the news.

"We have, this morning, discovered an issue" he said.

"An issue?" Nowell repeated, a questioning tone in his voice. He didn't like issues. Surprises even less. Issues caused problems, and he had no time for problems, especially not if they threatened to derail his business. Yet issues could be fixed. At least, he hoped they could.

Covell led him into a long room that housed nothing but a heavy table and a couple of chairs. Nowell's heart quickened in his chest as he entered to see something lying on the table, covered entirely by a red sheet of cloth. Covell invited him to inspect the object.

"As I said, an issue" he said quietly.

Nowell wondered why he was whispering – there was nobody else in the room, and whatever was beneath that sheet was clearly not going to be repeating anything. He walked slowly around the table, not really wanting to disturb the covering. He had little need to do so; just looking at it he knew it was. A body. The question was, whose? Covell pulled back the cloth slowly to reveal a haggard, elderly face, with wiry grey hair amassed at the top and snaking outward as though reaching for something unseen. Nowell shuddered. It was Old Demdike.

Her eyes were closed, for which Nowell was thankful, for he did not wish to look into the fading grey eyes of an alleged witch. Who knew what power they still retained, even after death? Certainly he didn't, and had no desire to find out.

"Found her this morning" Covell explained, his tone as matter-of-fact as if he were describing what he had eaten for breakfast.

"Must have gone overnight. The others didn't know either, until the guards pulled her out of the dungeon."

Nowell considered the other prisoners still held in the death-cell. He imagined her daughter cursing that her mother had escaped without her and left them to their fate, the granddaughter sobbing in the darkness, Chattox silently relishing the demise of her old adversary. Or perhaps she too felt the grief for a one-time friend now passed into eternity. It mattered not to him of course, for their anguish, or anger, was surely part of a fitting punishment for their crimes. The rest would come soon enough and, if all went well and he had his way, they would all be joining the old crone again presently anyway. He ordered the body to be recovered and disposed of at the earliest convenience – and with the utmost discretion. The last thing he needed was the resting place of Elizabeth Southern becoming some sort of shrine, or worse. There would be no sacred burial, no service, no mourners. Nothing to identify either her, or the place. Covell nodded his agreement and left to set the task in motion.

Roger Nowell regarded the remains for a moment before making his exit. Slowly he stalked away down the familiar corridors towards the courthouse to find the others, a renewed sense of urgency filling his mind. Things had to move, and quickly, before any more lives were lost in the underground prison. Death *would* claim these people, but not the natural kind of death. The gallows must end their lived. Justice must be seen to be done.

27

The six men sat in the courthouse in an uncomfortable silence. For a good few minutes nobody spoke, their minds brimming with the news they had just received. Elizabeth Southern – old Demdike – was dead. The main player in their crusade had cheated justice. Cheated them of the glory of her condemnation. The disappointment was rife, and very bitter.

Nowell pondered the situation. He had lost the lynchpin of his war – one of them at least, Chattox was still a viable and a possible major success – and had therefore failed in his quest. Surely the Court would not look favourably on such an event. The King wanted the dark arts eradicated, the users made examples of, and the message made clear across the nation. Magic, witchcraft, would *not* be tolerated in the kingdoms of James I. For the first time in a long while, he began to wonder exactly *why* the King felt the way he did. True, it was stated in the Bible, *Thou shalt not suffer a witch to live,* but he couldn't help but feel that there was much more to his seeming obsession with the subject. He sighed deeply. It was likely he would never know the answer to that question.

"So, what now?" a voice asked in the silence.

"Now, we continue our business". Nowell asserted, rising to his feet and straightening his cloak. "The old woman may have escaped earthly justice, but she shall not escape the justice of God himself. She shall face that now, and face it alone. We still have twenty other witches to deal with. The work goes on, gentlemen. The King desires us continue. The King *demands* it".

As though bolstered by Nowell's words, the other five men stood up almost simultaneously, their faces set with a steely determination. Nowell was, of course, correct. The investigation must continue to it's rightful conclusion.

Within the hour, eleven of the prisoners in the Well Tower Dungeon were herded into the courtrooms and forced to sit on the hard wooden benches that faced the judge's box. To their right were seated the men who were responsible for them being there- Nowell, Bannister, Wilsey, In front were three other men. One of them they each knew as Thomas Covell, the governor of their incarceration. The other two were strangers to them. At either end of the two benches were positioned two gaol guards, tasked with keeping them in some semblance or order. Eventually one of the strange men rose to his feet, silenced the room, and summoned Roger Nowell to the table. Nowell complied immediately.

"Are you ready to proceed in this matter?" he asked the magistrate. Nowell half turned and looked at the rabble behind him, a haughty and wry smile creeping across his face,

"Yes, Sir" he replied, returning his gaze to the man who had addressed him.

"Are all the documents ready?" the man continued.

"They are Sir".

The man nodded and dismissed Nowell back to his seat. For a moment he stood, reading the pages that lay on the desk, before raising his head and examining the wretches who had been brought into his courtroom. Witches, he thought to himself, surely these ragged people were not involved in such base activities? But then, he had heard tell that many such people were of a low born nature, just like these skin and boned folks. He could never quite understand why such people did not use their powers to make a better life for themselves – if they did indeed possess such powers. Stroking his heavy brown beard, he contemplated the questions that circled in his head. The alleged witches could do nothing but sit and wait for him to complete his musings. Finally he took a deep breath, shuffled the papers, and gave a loud cough to clear his throat. Being somewhat unconvinced of the case, he did not like what he was about to do, but the evidence he had seen up to this point suggested he had little other option. He motioned for the prisoners to stand.

Once each of the twenty people had staggered to their feet, he coughed once more and read out the list of names.

"Are all the aforementioned people here present?" he asked.

Nobody spoke until Nowell rose to his feet and gave the answer.

"Yes Sir. All present".

"Ladies and Gentlemen" he began. Nowell winced. The man was unrepentant. Regardless of their crimes, their *perceived* crimes, they were still people. They were still, at that moment, *innocent* people, and would remain so until proved and proclaimed otherwise by trial in court. They still deserved to be treated properly. In his court room, he would ensure that would happen.

"The King has declared a wish to see the elimination of witchcraft, magic and the dark arts.

You have been brought here in the belief that you are, or have practised such activities to a malignant end."

He paused.

"While I myself have some...concerns about the nature of such a case, it is my duty – to the King and to the Law – to inform you that you *shall* stand trial for the accusations levelled against you. The next proceedings in this area are in three months time. There, this matter shall be resolved. May God see that it be resolved in the correct way."

With that, he brought his gavel down onto the bench with a loud thump and stalked from the room, unable to shake the nagging feeling inside that the whole thing was a terrible mistake. There was nothing more he could do. He had done what had been required of him. May God have mercy on all of them.

28

Without hesitation, the crowd of now almost formally accused witches were ushered back to their underground confinement, and the door locked firmly behind them. Alison groped her way through the darkness, her hands stretched out before her until she fumbled against the moist masonry of the wall, her eyes stinging with the ever constant threat of salty tears, and she slid quickly down to the floor, her emaciated back scraping down the jagged stone. She felt the sharp pain as she went, yet somehow it did not seem to matter any more. Nothing mattered any more. It was over.

Somewhere opposite she could hear her brother muttering to himself. Alison closed her eyes and willed him be quiet. It didn't work. The indecipherable murmur continued, the speaker's voice low and raspy, and not at all the way that she remembered him to sound. But then, every one of them had changed since their arrival in that place – and not for the better either. Gone were her mother's plump arms and cheeks, replaced by a traceable network of bone and stringy flesh that only just seemed to cover them. Her voice too had been replaced by an exhausted growl. How she wished she could hear their old sounds again. She had never before imagined that she would miss being barked at for not collecting enough money that day, or being teased or insulted by her elder brother. She missed being rebuked by her now dead grandmother, who's words were enough to cut through even the thickest of skin. She even longed to hear Jennet's annoying, childish babble and endless questions. Jennet. She had hardly considered her younger sister since her removal almost two months previously. Silently she wondered what had happened to the youngster, whose entire kin were now either dead or locked in that dungeon. Where was she now? It took a good few minutes for her to realise that she was crying.

"...when we get 'ome".

She heard James finish a previously unheard sentence.

"What do ye mean, when we get 'ome?"

her mother snapped from somewhere in the room.

"What I said. I'm a gonna get us some nice fresh mutton when we get 'ome. The King's business will be o'er soon and we can go 'ome"

Alison felt as though her head was about to explode. Instead it was her voice that did so.

"Don't be a fool, Jam" she hissed. "There ain't gonna be no mutton, nor lamb, nor any goin' 'ome for that. We are going to trial. Ain't no way out for us now!"

"But the King..."

She didn't allow him to finish.

"The King nowt" she half shouted into the void between them. "*This* is the King's business. It's the King's business that we are all gonna 'ang, and make no mistake".

An abrupt silence enveloped the room. No more words were spoken. The only sounds to be heard were the unwanted combination of scurrying rats and muffled sobbing. Alison turned her body to face in the opposite direction and went to sleep.

29

Days went by and weeks passed without any of them seeing so much as a glimpse of daylight, or of the world that went on outside the circular Well Tower dungeon. Food was a rarity, meaning that James and some of the other less fussy occupants had taken to killing and eating the rats that also considered the place home. Despite the deep rumbling that frequently emanated from her ever decreasing stomach, Alison refused to even contemplate such a revolting suggestion, and continued to go without. James called her a fool. Perhaps she was. A tired, hungry, hopeless fool.

Finally they came.

The guards. In their flailing cloaks and heavy boots. Thumping down the steps and through the door to haul their captives to their feet and out to their fate.

Again, they were instructed to be seated on the same uncomfortable wooden benches as on their last visit to the courtroom, half of them on one set, the others immediately opposite. Two chairs were set in the Judge's Box, with several others accompanying them at a slightly lower level. Alison stared around the wooden panelled room, a lump forming at the back of her already parched throat. Timidly she reached for her mother's hand, only to be denied the comfort by the older woman snatching hers away before contact was made. That was it then. At that moment, Alison was made all to aware that she was facing the uncertainty completely alone.

A fanfare blared from the rear of the room, causing her to half jump in surprise. The guards ushered them to their feet as the doors opened to admit five men, all of them dressed in similar white tunics and red cloaks, all of them taking their places with a distinct lack of expression on their rather similar faces. Behind them followed two more gentlemen, obviously of far more importance than their predecessors, garbed in tunics of heavy black and robes of deep Scarlett, with trimmings of white around the edges. They approached the two prominent chairs, instructed the room to be seated, and sat down.

The courtroom was full. Word of the possible witches had travelled fast and far and, the assizes being entirely public spectacles, many had come to view these malignant creatures for themselves. Alison recognised some of them as she scanned the crowd. Some were family members of those believed to have been maimed or murdered by witchcraft, including Abraham Lawe whom she spotted at the centre back of the room. Others were just people out for a day's entertainment. All were seemingly eager to begin.

One of the two prominent men rose to his feet and introduced himself loudly as Judge Bromley, before reading aloud from the document he held in this fat, white hand.

"The Assizes here held" he began with as much pomp as he could muster, "are to determine the evidence presented in cases of witchcraft, and the accused witches as followeth".

He paused and glared around the room.

"Elizabeth Southern" he boomed, "It is my understanding that this woman hath died before trial. Is that correct?"

"Correct, Sir" Nowell called from the floor.

"In which case, God himself shall be her Judge" Bromley went on, dismissing old Demdike from his thoughts.

"Elizabeth Device. Stand." Elizabeth obeyed.

"Are you guilty or nor guilty of the crimes with which you are now charged?"

"Not guilty" she announced in a confident voice.

"Sit". Bromley instructed. Elizabeth quickly took her seat.

He then proceeded to recite the names of the defendants, in a kind of macabre roll call until all twenty names had been called, and twenty pleas had been noted.

"Let it be known, here and now, that the King will not tolerate any instances of witchcraft in his kingdoms. Such activities will be stamped out, and the perpetrators dealt with in a swift and decisive manner". Bromley's voice travelled authoritatively around the room. Alison listened to his words, unsure as to exactly what he meant, but sure that, whatever their meaning, they didn't sound good.

"And with that" the judge continued, "let the proceedings commence!"

Nowell strutted into the centre of the floor, his heeled boots clattering beneath him as he paraded from one side of the room to the other, staring continuously at his prey as he passed. Only Alison flinched beneath his gaze, her head lowering as he set his eyes on her. Nowell smiled to himself. She was a scared little girl, and he had her in exactly the spot he wanted her to be. He held his position in front of her for what seemed like an eternity before returning his attentions to the two judges who waited patiently for him to begin.

"A fortnight ago" the magistrate began, addressing the crowd rather than the judges, "a woman was tried at the Assizes in York on charges of witchcraft. A woman who had bewitched to death a man by the name of Thomas Lister, and had caused great loss to Mr Leonard Lister, his kinsman. This woman had previously been tried, and acquitted of the murder of a child. A CHILD".

He stressed the last two words loudly, as though hoping they would have the maximum impact on the listeners. Loud gasps emanated from somewhere in the crowd.

"On this second charge, pertaining to the unfortunate Mr Listers, she was convicted. She went to the gallows two days later and paid for her crimes. Her name: Jennet Preston".

The three members of the Device family stared straight ahead, hardly daring to make any movement. They didn't even dare glance in one another's direction. Alison shuffled on her seat. James swallowed hard. Jennet Preston was an old friend of Elizabeth's from many years ago. Jennet Preston had been in their home on that Good Friday that had started all this. Jennet Preston had been executed as a witch. Things were going from bad to worse.

"We know all that, Mr Nowell" Judge Altham interjected. "We sat as judges on those Assizes also. It was we who passed the sentence upon her. The question here is, what is the relevance of Jennet Preston to *this* case?"

"Well, Sir" Nowell bowed with a sycophantic smile. "I have here documented evidence that that same Jennet Preston was a close associate of at least some of the accused here today. That she was present at a covern held at the home of Elizabeth Device and her kin on the Good Friday just passed".

Altham stroked his stubbled chin and considered the statement. A link between the two cases was surely both interesting and exceptionally concerning. If true, it suggested that this connected group of witches stretched much further than had been previously anticipated.

"We shall take all that into consideration in due course, Mr Nowell" said Bromley, seizing up a parchment of paper that lay before him.

"Until then, there is another piece of important business I must conduct before we continue. Will Jane Southworth, Jennet Brierley and Eileen Brierley please stand up".

A murmur rose across the benches as the three women rose unsteadily to their feet.

"Jane Southworth, Jennet Brierley and Eileen Brierley, you have been charged by the authorities of Samlesbury, with the atrocities of witchcraft, murder and cannibalism. Of using diverse devilish and wicked Arts, called Witchcrafts, Enchantments, Charmes, and Sorceries, in and upon one Grace Sowerbutts. Heinous accusations which, if true, will immediately convey your souls to the Devil himself."

He paused. The three Samlesbury women waited for him to continue, their faces clouded with fear of condemnation.

"You may be seated while we hear the testimony of Miss Grace Sowerbutts".

Grace came forward from the gallery and was directed into the witness box. She was a young girl, of around fourteen years of age, with long red hair, freckles and uneven eyes of a muddy brown colour that seemed too big for the face around them.

"State your name" Altham said sharply, before adding a rather apologetic, "please".

The child confirmed her name.

"What is your relationship to the defendants?"

"She's my Aunt" she said, pointing at the Brierley women in turn, "and she's my grandmother".

Thomas Potts scribbled furiously on his parchment.

"And what have you come here today to tell us, child?" Bromley spoke so softly he was hardly recognisable as the booming voice from moments earlier.

Grace looked at the two women and breathed deeply.

"That they are witches, Sir".

The crowd gasped in unison.

"Witches?" Nowell repeated gently, inviting her to continue. Grace took the bait.

"Aye, Sir. Haunted and tormented me all my life they have. They tried to make me thrown myself in the well, and once they were going to throw me from atop the hayrigg by my hair. They make them clay figure and stick pins in them to hurt people. Me included. Why, the broke my arm by pulling a piece of the figure away from its body, so they did."

"Why would they wish harm to come to you, Grace? Their own granddaughter, and niece?"

"Didn't want me around Sir. Because I said I would tell on them if they didn't stop. But they didn't listen, Sir. They never listen. And then they stole the baby".

"What baby, Grace?"

"The Walshman baby. They took it from its crib, and sucked its blood. Stuck a needle in its leg, Sir. They put it back, but it died next day Sir. Then they went at night to the churchyard and took the body away."

"What happened to the body?"

"They ate it, Sir. Well, parts of it. Used some of it to make potions to change themselves into other things".

"Such as what?"

"Dogs, and horses, and even birds, Sir".

"And you have seen this with your own eyes?"

"Aye Sir. I used to follow them sometimes, down to Red Bank, where they met with four strange, black things. Like men, but not men. foure black things, going upright, and yet not like men in the face. I don't know what they are, Sir, but they come to the Red Bank, and feast, and join with writhing bodies on the ground, with lots of moaning and screaming to be heard."

"How many times did this happen?"

"Lots, Sir. I stopped following after a while. I was scared of what was happening, and that they might make me join in if they knew I was there. So I didn't go no more. Thought it were safer that way, Sir".

Altham nodded his agreement and dismissed her from the seat. She returned to the gallery, passing the bench which held her relatives, with a pleased smirk on her face as she retook her place.

"Calling Mr Thomas Walshman to the stand, please".

The slender figure of Mr Walshman glided to the witness box, his shoulders haunched, his head bowed, a folded white handkerchief in his right hand. He fought back tears as he recounted the death of his only child on that cold March night, the one year old boy taking his last breath in his father's arms after they had found him shaking in his cot only an hour previously.

The doctors had been unable to explain what had ailed the child so suddenly, and had recorded the death as of unknown causes. Asked about the events of the night before, Walshman confirmed that the child had gone missing from his bed for about an hour and a half, during which time a frantic search was being carried out by himself and his wife. The child had reappeared in the bed when they returned.

"And you believe he was taken, and then returned?"

"A one year old child does not disappear from a high sided crib by his own devices Sir. Nor does he simply vanish and climb right back in while you're searching".

"No, indeed Mr Walshman. I guess he does not!" Bromley acquiesced. "When he returned, was he marked in any way?".

Walshman thought for a moment.

"There was an odd marking on his leg, I did notice. Looked like a pin prick, or just slightly larger. He was awfully white too, as though the colour had been taken from his cheeks".

The two judges exchanged glances.

Two more witnesses came forward to tell the court that Jane Southworth was an evil woman, intent on doing harm, and that her own father in law refused to go anywhere near the house because of her foul nature. When all the Samlesbury witnesses had been heard, Bromley asked the women what answer they could give to the charges and evidence laid against them. As one, the three women fell to their knees, hot tears running down their faces.

"It isn't true" Eileen Brierley protested, in broken speech.

"It's all lies" added her mother, "Please, Sir, if not for ours, then for God's cause please examine Grace Sowerbutts. We beg of you, please".

At once, Grace Sowerbutt's expression changed. Her face turned a ghostly shade of white, and she began chewing on her bottom lip until small drops of blood bubbled on its surface.

"We have heard her testimony" Bromley stated firmly, "and yet I am minded to hear it a second time".

Grace turned to the man seated to her left.

"I told you this wasn't going to work" she hissed.

"I said it was a bad idea from the start" he whispered back. "It was you who wanted to do it. You insisted on taking the stand".

"I did as I was told" she rejoined, stroppily.

"What's going on back there?" Bromley thundered, his fists banging down on the wood of his desk.

"Told, by whom?" asked one of the five jurors, who was close enough to hear the exchange.

Grace and the man stared at each other, the realisation that they had been caught out dawning quickly in their minds. Altham repeated the question.

"Told what, by whom?"

"Grace is only a child Sir. A simple child. She only did as she was told by the Priest, Thompson."

The crowd began to chatter loudly. Bromley silenced them with another beat of his fist.

"The child shall be re-examined" he declared. "But not here. There is little time for this. Mr Leigh and Mr Chisnal shall take her to the other court house, along with Mr Wilsey. They shall determine the truth of the matter and report back to us." With that, the weeping child was led from the courtroom by the three men designated with her care, the two judges swept out of the doors and the accused were left in the courtroom, with the guards, to wonder what might happen next.

30

They didn't have to wait for long. Less than an hour later, the court was reconvened, Grace and her examiners were readmitted to the proceedings, and the child's statement was submitted. Bromley read the statement aloud.

"I, Grace Sowerbutt's, do recount the testimony given in this courtroom here today" he read, casting her a firm glance over the rim of his spectacles.

"The story I told was untrue, in every aspect except for the fact that the accused are, indeed, my aunt and grandmother. I was told what I should say about them by the Priest in the Hall at Samlesbury, who promised me that God would love me if I should do as he say. That my mother would come back for me, and all would be well.

I make humble apology for the untruths I have told, and ask forgiveness for my sins.

Grace Sowerbutts. Aged 14 years."

Bromley held the paper in the air.

"Is this your name written at the bottom, Grace?"

"Yes Sir".

"And do you now declare, before the court, that this statement be the truth?"

"Aye Sir, I do".

Bromley placed the paper down and called forth the three women. Jane Southworth admitted that the Jesuit priest who had taken refuge and the chaplaincy in the Hall at Samlesbury, was her husband's uncle, and that he was currently going by the name of Thompson in order to avoid detection. Grace confirmed that this was the man who had instructed her original testimony. Not one of the three women, nor the remorseful child, were able to provide a reason for his actions, other than the fact that they all attended the Anglican, rather than the Jesuit Church. None could swear as to whether that be the cause and, in his absence, no other motive could be determined. Bromley returned his spectacles to the bridge of his nose and turned to the jury.

"We have heard today a good example of how the law can be manipulated for the gain of others" he sighed, "and how easily lies can be told. The child has readily admitted to telling untruths against her kin, a crime in itself and not easily justified in any situation. However, she has set the matter straight before it became too late. Therefore, in the matter of the case against Jane Southworth, Eileen Brierley and Jennet Brierley, I instruct you to find the defendants not guilty".

He turned to the three trembling women.

"God hath delivered you beyond expectation" he told them. "I pray God you may use this mercy and favour well; and take heed you fall not hereafter: And so the court doth order that you shall be delivered from this place, as were the five others arrested alongside you, and be released with no mark against your name or person. God speed you".

Jane Southworth, Jennet Brierley and her daughter were led out, through the clamour of the crowded courthouse and into the corridor beyond. From there they were whisked quickly through the castle complex and out of the main doors, their freedom at last ensured. Grace and her male companion also departed, albeit in a different direction, spirited away from the scene by their carriage and horses and back towards Samlesbury. Alison sat back on the bench and contemplated the events of the morning. Surely now there was some tiny glimmer of hope for herself and her kin. Closing her eyes, she grasped that tiny glimmer with all her might. There was still a chance.

31

"Anne Whittle, step forwards".

The voice brought Alison firmly back into the courtroom as the eighty year old woman, with the ratty grey hair and stooped back, whom the majority of people knew solely as Old Chattox, gingerly pulled herself to her feet and approached the bar that separated the benches and the main floor. Bromley waited for her to steady herself before reading aloud the charges against her; namely that of slaying one Robert Nutter by the foul means of witchcraft, and asked her how she did plead.

"Not guilty" she croaked, staring motionlessly at the two men who dared to sit in judgement of her. Only Bromley returned her gaze. Or what he believed was her gaze for, as it turned out, Anne Whittle was almost completely blind.

Roger Nowell once more took the floor, pacing back and forth before the gentlemen of the jury as though deep in thought, his mind whirring with the determination that success would be his. He had watched in horror as the three Samlesbury women had been exonerated, just as he had when their five companions had been dismissed a few weeks earlier. He had listened in disbelief when another of his prey had been sentenced only to being pilloried on four market days – one each in the towns of Clitheroe, Whalley, Padiham and Lancaster - with a piece of paper making public her offence. Nowell took small comfort in the conviction, nor of the fact that a year of imprisonment followed for Margaret Pearson. She had escaped the gallows and therefore, in his eyes, she had escaped the King's justice. Two women had now scuppered his quest; he would not allow any more to go free. He was determined. Starting with the aged Anne Whittle, these remaining prisoners were going to be his glorification.

"Mrs Whittle" he began, after a period of quiet so long that the interruption made the woman half jump on the spot.

"Are you a witch?"

"No, Sir. I am not!"

"Hmm" Nowell hummed as he turned away from her.

"Members of the Jury, we shall now hear the evidence against this woman".

Nowell recounted to the avidly attentive audience, information that he had gleaned from James during the months of interviews; that on the All Hallow's Eve of the previous year, Anne Whittle had been sitting before a huge fire, telling stories to the folks of the Hill. She had been seated, according to the Device lad, where the flickering flames had thrown menacing shadows around her, so that she appeared phantom-like to the already afeared youngsters, the crackling of the wood adding a second layer of horror to her words. She had told tales of bogarts running wild on the hillside, terrorising all that crossed their paths and causing mayhem in the fields. She had talked of spirits and ghosts, witches and demons, sacrifices and possessions. Filled them with near dread, James had added with a shudder. When pressed more by his interrogators, James recounted the story she had told about Richard Baldwin of Pendle.

It was the last tale of the night he had said, as a reasoning for it being the one he remembered the most, and that a glazed look had come over her face as she was speaking the words, almost as though she was reliving rather than inventing the narrative. She had talked of how a *Thing like a Christian man* had visited her on regular occasions and asked her for her soul. After a few years of resisting, she had surrendered, on the promise that she should lack nothing, and would get any revenge she wanted. The *thing* had instructed her to call him by the name of Fancy -which she had thought a peculiar name for such a man – and had made a request of his own. That she should help him hurt the wife of Richard Baldwin. Whittle had refused to agree to this condition. She had no quarrel with the Baldwins, and therefore could not think of a reason for her to do anything of the kind. She had, she had said, enquired as to Fancy's reasons for his request, but had been met with a moment's cold silence and an unspoken refusal to answer. The creature had then lunged at her and attempted to pierce the skin of her arm with his teeth. He managed only to make contact with the cows-hide sleeve of her clothing. She had been too afraid to ask a second time.

The All Hallow's Eve tale had then gone on to talk about how this same Fancy had encouraged her to take revenge upon Robert Nutter for his threat to expel her family from the land upon which they lived, should it ever pass through the family into his possession, because her daughter had rejected the man's improper attentions. Nutter had died suddenly some three months later. To add more thrill to her seasonal words, she told how Fancy liked to appear in the form of a large brown bear, or as a striding lion to frighten the folks for his own merriment, adding a note of caution to her listeners that they should not roam far on the hillside after the fall of darkness for fear they should meet and fall prey to one of Fancy's tricks. It had stuck in his head, James had told Nowell, and from that moment he had been reluctant to be out of doors after sundown.

Nowell paused to allow the audience to consider the statement. Chattox stood at the bar, her whole body wanting to cry out that she had been telling a *story*, a simple, made up story for the hill folk on All Hallow's Eve. Such things happened on the hill every year at that time. The words are not real. She knew, however, that to speak out would be a grave mistake, and that she would not be heard even should she attempt to do so. They had been told on their arrival at the courthouse that they would not be allowed to speak for themselves, save for answering the few questions directed straight at them. On no terms were any of them permitted to interrupt the proceedings. They were to sit, listen and accept their fate.

Nowell then went on to read out the statement regarding the stealing of skulls and teeth from the New Church, and the accusations of clay effigies and muttered curses. Again, Chattox had to stop herself from reminding him that these 'curses' were actually the prayers of the Old Religion of the area. Again, she remembered that to do so would not serve to help her cause. Again, she remained silent.

In time, Nowell concluded his evidence against Anne Whittle, stated as much to the judges, and she was dismissed back to the benches, to be replaced by the limping figure of Elizabeth Device. She shuffled forwards, ignoring the gasps, sniggers and whispers of the crowd – many of whom had never set eyes on her before today, and were appalled, or amused, by her shorter right leg and her unevenly placed eyes. Accustomed to a lifetime of such reactions, Elizabeth paid no heed, taking her place before the men who would decide her fate.

Nowell accepted her plea of innocence and again read out the evidence against the accused. Throughout the day he repeated this sequence with the statements against James Device and the first of two indictments against Anne Redfern, before turning at last to the events that had started his pursuit almost five months previously. This was where he finally nailed his case, and these witches, to the stake. Or, to be more precise, to the gallows.

Alison Device crept timidly towards the bar, her previously attractive features now greatly diminished by the ravages of hunger, grime and lack of daylight. Nowell grinned triumphantly at the sight of the young, terrified girl before him; if the appearances of these people didn't convince the court of their guilt, nothing would. All he needed to do was call the main witness, the crowning jewel, the one and only Mr Abraham Lawe.

And so it was that the eagerly listening crowd, the jury and the two judges heard of the events that had taken place at Colne Edge on that early March morning. They learned of Alison's encounter with John Lawe, the simple peddler man who was out trying to make an honest living when he was accosted by a young girl who wanted some pins from him. They were told how Mr Lawe had refused to open his bag, knowing that this child did not possess the ability to pay for the goods, and how the girl had shouted curses at him for not heeding her request, causing the man to collapse onto the ground and need urgent medical assistance. When asked about his father's illness, Abraham spared no details in his account of how the old man had foamed at the mouth, lost the power of his tongue and had been unable to stand on his own two legs. Nowell savoured every word.

"And where is your father now?" Bromley asked, once Abraham had completed his tale.

"At home in Halifax, Sir. He is still very weak, the doctors say he will always be so now, since..."

Abraham cast a sullen look in Alison's direction. The girl lowered her head, unable to meet his eyes.

"They said he wasn't well enough to come here today". Abraham turned his face back to the judges. "That is why I am here, to represent my father in this matter."

He nodded his head firmly, as if that was all he had to say on the subject. He thought it prudent not to add the fact that his father, though decidedly still suffering from his affliction, had steadfastly *refused* to attend the trial of his attacker. He had actually *forgiven* the girl for her part in the events. Didn't wish to see her punished, so he did not. No, the court shall not hear of that, for it could well change the outcome of the hearing, and that could not be allowed to happen. The old man may have forgiven, but he, Abraham, most definitely had not.

"The girl whom you say cursed your father" Bromley continued, "is she in this room here today?"

"Yes Sir"

"Can you identify her for the Court, please?"

"Yes Sir" he said, turning slowly to his left and pointing his long, thin finger in Alison's direction. "It is her. Alison Device. She tried to kill my father!".

Loud whisperings filled the room as the crowd took in the damning testimony. Nowell remained silent. Abraham glared coldly at Alison, who did not raise her head, keeping her eyes firmly on her feet as the judge's gavel once more made contact with the bench.

"Quiet" Bromley shouted, eager to maintain control over the proceedings.

"Or I shall have to remove you from the room".

The murmurings subsided immediately. Nobody wanted to miss the rest of the show.

"Thank you, Mr Lawe. You may now step down".

Abraham stepped away from the stand. A moment's peace settled as Bromley and Altham considered the next move. Papers shuffled on the desk. Bottoms shuffled on the benches. An air of expectation hung in the room. Eventually, Altham raised his head and placed his spectacles back onto his nose.

"The Court will now hear from Jennet Device".

32

Jennet Device walked to the front of the courtroom with a poise and confidence that made her seem much more advanced in years than her age suggested. All three remaining family members turned as she was called, a look of confusion in their faces; surely she was not going to speak against her own kin? Elizabeth made to stand as her youngest child passed the bench, resuming her seated position as Alison pulled on her arm with a shake of her head. Jennet did not look at her mother, or her siblings, concentrating as she was on the task before her. Bromley leaned forward across his desk to look at her.

"It appears that from here, we are unable to see the witness" he said. "Mr Nowell, can we set the maid upon a table in the presence of the Court?"

Jennet did not need to be asked twice. Quick as a hare she scrambled up onto the desk where Nowell was standing and straightened her skirt with the palms of her hand."

"Better, Sir?" she asked.

"Much" he replied. "Now then. Who are you?"

"Jennet, Sir. Jennet Device".

Another murmur circled the room. While Device was her given name, it was well known that old John Device had died in the year the child had been born, his final illness surely rendering him incapable of being the baby's natural parent. Elizabeth heard the whispers and began to breathe deeply. She must control her temper.

"Jennet, are any of these people your relatives?" Nowell began his questioning of the witness.

"Aye Sir, that one's my ma, and there's ma bruvver and sister", she pointed them out with her finger.

"And you live with these people I presume?"

"Aye, Sir. And Me Gramma. Well, I did Sir, until you took 'em away".

"And do you know why they were taken away, child?"

"Aye Sir. Cos of the witch blood".

Bromley slowly peeled his spectacles down his nose and peered over their rim. Altham sat back in his seat. Nowell had stopped walking. This was new. Not once in the whole case had anyone ever used that phrase. He had heard it before, a long time ago, when folklore and legend talked about magic being a part of a bloodline, a trait

passed down through the generations like nobility or disease. Dismissed throughout history as stuff and nonsense, Nowell now began to wonder. Could witch blood actually be a real thing? How would a child know about it otherwise? He decided to push the subject further.

"Witch blood, Jennet?"

"Aye Sir. It's magic that's in the blood Sir. Part of who you are, part of your kin. Ye cant escape havin' it, but ye can choose how ye use it!.

"Is the witch blood in your kin, Jennet?"

Jennet considered her reply carefully. They may accuse her of being a witch too if she were not careful. Fortunately she had been thinking about this subject for quite some time.

"Aye Sir. In some of 'em. My Gramma had it. Got it from her Pa I think. She taught me Ma how to use it, and then they both taught Alison and James."

"Did they teach you, Jennet?"

"No, Sir. They never teach me nowt. I ain't worth owt to 'em Sir. I'm an outsider, so I ain't important.

So even if it be in me blood, I ain't knowing how to do owt wi' it".

"But you are their kin, Jennet. They love you"

Jennet snorted at the suggestion.

"I were a *sin*, Sir. A mistek, if e'er she med one. She told me oft enough. All of 'em did".

Elizabeth jumped to her feet, this time before Alison was able to stop her from doing so.

"Ye fibbin' little rat" she hissed. The child cowered on the table behind Nowell. She wasn't really frightened, but she might as well make it look so.

"Ye know that ain't the truth, so why ye standin' there talkin' such rot?"

"Quiet please, Mrs Device" Altham reprimanded her. Elizabeth's nostrils flared, but she said nothing more. Altham turned his attentions back to the child.

"So your mother uses the witch blood?"

"Aye Sir. They all do. I know 'bout it cos I heard me Ma and Gramma talkin' bout it in th' firehouse one day. About usin' it to smite someone for summat. I ain't knowin' what tho".

Again, her mother shot to her feet.

"Ye little snake" she shouted. "After everythin' we done fer ye. Kept ye, loved ye, begged and borrowed so as we could feed n' dress ye, we did. Ye ungrateful wench, i'll see thee done fer this, so I will".

"Remove that woman!" Altham roared to the guards at the door. "I will not tolerate this in my courtroom!"

Elizabeth was dragged from the benches and out of the doors, her face turned always towards the still cowering child, her lips moving in silent speech. The doors slammed behind them. Alison and James exchanged a brief glance between themselves. They knew that that was not going to help.

Her mother removed from view, Jennet Device once more found her confidence. At least she pretended to.

"Remember what we agreed?" Nowell whispered, in the pretence of comforting the apparently terrified child.

"Of course" she whispered back. "I help ye, and ye'll help me find me favver".

"I shall endeavour to try, at least" he said.

Jennet didn't know what that meant, but she was satisfied with the sound of it.

"Are you ready to continue?" Altham asked gently. Jennet took a deep intake of breath and nodded.

For the next hour or so, Jennet Device regaled the court with the best tales of magic and malice that her eleven year old imagination had been able to come up with; some of it based on true events, most of it dreamt up over the time spent waiting for this moment. She told of the deaths of John and James Robinson, who had been involved in a dispute with her mother, and of Henry Mitton, who refused to give her a penny when asked. She told of meetings at Malkin Tower, and dances around firepits, of cavorting with strange creatures in the black of night, and suddenly appearing dogs, cats and other animals, who could all talk with her mother, grandmother, brother and sister. She mentioned the Good Friday meeting at her home, and pointed out all the accused that had been present. The court was captivated by both this brown haired, freckled girl and her fantastical stories. Not a sound was to be heard when Jennet Device finished her statement.

At length she was done. Nowell lifted her down from the table and set her on the floor with a sly smile and nod of his head. The child gave him a mischievous wink and made her exit.

Elizabeth Device was thrust back through the doors some minutes following the departure of her daughter. Nowell stepped up to the judges and communicated with them in hushed tones, before giving them a slight bow and taking his seat. Altham signalled for the gentlemen of the jury to stand, following which he instructed them to go out to an adjoining room and come to a conclusion regarding the guilt, or innocence, of the three members of the Device family, Anne Whittle and Anne Redfern. The judges left for their chambers, Nowell flounced out of the doors and the prisoners were left to ponder their futures.

That evening, the congregation piled back into the courtroom to hear the verdicts. Anne Whittle was the first called. She hardly seemed to react as the word *guilty* was announced, clear as it had been to her that that would be the only outcome of the trial. Elizabeth Device hissed as she received her condemnation. Anne Redfern listened as James and Alison were convicted of witchcraft and malevolent acts against others, before stepping forward to receive her own verdict.

"Not guilty".

Anne Redfern let out a loud sob as she heard the words; whether it was a sob of relief for herself, or of lament for her convicted mother she wasn't quite sure. She staggered back to her seat, to be greeted with a smile by the elderly Chattox. They sat, together as they had throughout the ordeal, hand in hand, the mother tenderly stroking her child's wasted hand. Chattox was full aware that this could be their last communion. Her sands of time were running low. Her Annie had been reprieved; that was all that mattered to her now.

33

Alison slept more that night than she had done in the time since her unfortunate encounter with the peddler, John Lawe. She dreamed that she was walking on Pendle once more. The grass was green and dew-washed, and almost up to her ankles in height as she wandered lazily through the fields. A hare scampered across her path and into the clumps of bushes and trees, it's cloudy tail the last thing to disappear from view. A deer the colour of milk stopped to look at her over its shoulder as she approached, its mud brown eyes never wavering until the sound of dogs in the distance frightened it into a rapid departure. Alison watched it bound away, wishing she was as free as he.

The hills began to dissolve around her, melting into the darkening purple sky like smoke from a fire pit. Rain began to fall; rain unlike anything she had ever seen before, descending in large black spots that pooled on the path, one after the other in a line that appeared to lead into the distance. Reluctantly she found herself following the trail. On and on it went, taking her past Malkin Tower and Bull Hole Farm. Up the hillside, along a pathway that brought her to a large house not too dissimilar to Read Hall, with its fine gardens and ivy trailed walls. As she stood looking at the building, confused for she knew that it did not really stand in that spot, Alison was certain she had seen something in one of the upstairs windows. A slight trace of movement, the gentle flap of a red curtain. A dog brushed her leg; she bent to pat the brown and white animal, who wagged its tail at her and moved off to examine something further off. She pulled herself upwards. There is was again, at the window, a face. She knew that face. It was her sister, Jennet, half hidden by the lattice work of the window, her mousy hair now trussed up into ringlets and black ribbons. Alison raised a hand in acknowledgement. Jennet looked right through her, instead staring down at her one time sister with a face as hard as stone. Suddenly she reached up and snatched the curtains shut, leaving Alison alone on the road once more. Alison's eyes filled with tears. Even in her dreams her little sister had forsaken her.

She awoke with a start, her flailing legs pulling at the iron ring in the centre of the floor to which each of the prisoners was fastened.

"What ye callin' on that wretch fer?" she heard her mother murmur as she shuffled at her side. "She 'trayed us all. That rat ain't gonna help ye, that much is clear. Ain't no one gonna help us now".

Alison sighed and closed her eyes, once more drifting off into her wandering slumber. She was again on the hillside, pursuing the raindrops which continued to descend, although when she checked herself she was surprised to find that she wasn't at all wet. Not even damp. Read Hall had vanished now, leaving nothing but a desolate view of Pendle in its place. The trees were bare, their limbs reaching out as though they would grab her as she passed. Huge black birds circled overhead, their cries louder than her ears could stand as they swooped and dived against the violet sky. She felt suddenly very scared. Alison had never felt scared out here, on the hillside that she had always called home, but now – now a strange terror possessed her. The wind howled, bending the branches in a way that looked like they were showing her the way she must go. Her heart racing, she tried to turn back, only to discover that her feet would not move. No attempts to make herself walk were successful. She had two options: stay where she was, or continue the way she had been going. She decided on the latter.

Up the incline she trudged, the stones jagged and rough beneath her bare feet, past the entrances to Moss End, and WellField, and over the stile that she used to play on as a child with her friends, Meg and Jane. Roughlee Hall, again appearing a good distance from where it actually stood, loomed into view, and further off, the dwellings at Crowtrees, opposite the free flowing stream that now seemed to bubble like a cauldron to her right. The large farmhouse stood before her. Alison shuddered at the sight of the once proud home of Alice Nutter and her family, now left to decay and ruin. The door lay on the ground as though it had been pulled from its resting place with force, the building bleak, deserted and half demolished – by the elements or by human hand she was unable to decipher. Alice would be devastated to see her beloved home in such a state. And where where her family? Her son, Miles, who should have been continuing the work during his mother's absence. Where was he? It took Alison a moment to remember that Alice was, like her, a suspected witch. If found guilty, her lands would be confiscated to the Crown, her family forcibly removed. She closed her eyes and remembered better days. On she went, through the sparse fields and overgrown heather patches, past dense bushes and hedgerows, peat bogs and jagged rocks. The climb was steeper than she remembered it to be; her heart thumped against her ribcage and she struggled to catch her breath, stopping every now and then to aid the sharp pain that was developing in her side. The wind whipped around her in a sudden gust, almost knocking her slender body to the ground in its wake. She reached out for the thick branch of the nearest tree to steady herself. The sky brightened, and then plunged to a sinister deep purple, the echoes of the screaming birds continuing to resonate across the open space as she began to pull at an invisible force that seemed to be constricting her throat. Small, crescent shaped marks furrowed into flesh as she clawed at her neck in desperation, but there was nothing there to remove. Still, she could feel it, tightening quickly, her eyes beginning to feel as though they would explode at any given moment. Alison dropped to her knees, the grass hard and cold beneath her skin. She couldn't scream; the sounds just would not come forth.

The maroon sky swirled above her head. The trees, the bushes, the barely visible outline of buildings far into the distance faded rapidly into the vortex. Only the cacophony of the birds remained. Alison pressed her eyes closed, a feeling of absolute terror gripping her as she clung to the ground in fear for her life. Nothing stirred; she was not torn from her position and thrown into some awful abyss like the maelstrom threatened, nor did anything reach out and grab her while she lay, almost prostrate on the ground. Gradually she began to open her eyes. All that remained before her now was a soundless hillside. Not the Pendle hillside that she knew so well; this one was barren, the land scorched and laid to waste by some unseen hand. At the top was a structure of some kind, though she was unable to see it clearly from where she was. She wanted to go back, retreat down the path as quickly as she could, yet some form of strange fascination compelled her to rise up and move forwards, her bare feet scratching on the rough, uneven ground. And then, there it was; the two tall pieces of wood that towered up towards the slowly quietening sky, a third length lying horizontally over the top and covering the space in between. From the top portion there descended five pieces of what looked like rope, fashioned into circles, and hanging quite some distance from the ground. Alison swung herself round, almost certain that somebody, something, was behind her. She was alone. One singular bird cawed above her head, its cry sounding both ominous and cautionary in equal measure. Her breath hitched as she attempted to steady her breathing, the tightening sensation returning in her throat. And then, everything went black.

A bright light pierced her eyes. Alison roused herself from her sleep to find Covell and his men standing at the foot of the stairwell, a lighted rush in their hands.

"Rise and shine" his voiced boomed.

"Nutter, Hewitt, Bulcocks. Time to go."

The four named parties climbed unsteadily to their feet as one of the guards unchained their feet from the ring. They were ushered towards the door, John Bulcock muttering loudly about justice and lies, and protesting his innocence the entire time he could be heard, his mother making half hearted attempts to quieten him. Covell circled the remaining prisoners, all of whom were now officially convicted witches.

"Anne Redfern, its time to go!" he boomed, seemingly out of nowhere. Anne jumped.

"Am I free to go?" she asked, timidly.

"You are going" he snapped, "but free is not the word I'd be using. Off back to the Court you're going!"

Alison sat bolt upright, as did the others. Anne trembled with confusion as her chain was unlocked.

"I...I don't understand. I was found not guilty Sir. Yesterday. Cleared, I was. I ain't no witch. Court said so itself."

"I know nothing of that" Covell replied, hoisting her towards the exit. "All I know is you've been summoned back before the Judges, and that is exactly where you are going. Now!"

And with that, Anne Redfern was removed from the tower.

Back in the Courthouse, Anne was unceremoniously dumped before the Judges and Jury for a second time, on this occasion charged with the murder of Christopher Nutter, some nineteen years earlier. As she had on the previous day, she entered a plea of innocence. Nowell pompously read out a flurry of statements regarding clay images, enchantments and curses, yet provided no motive that would have enticed Anne to murder a man she barely knew. After only ten minutes, the case against her was heard and she was dismissed from the bar.

The statements against Katherine Hewitt, and John and Jane Bulcock were also brief – the primary witness once more appearing to be the ever willing Jennet Device, who picked each of them out as being present at the Good Friday meet at Malkin Tower. John Bulcock began to protest, but his words fell upon deaf ears. They too were dismissed to await their verdicts.

The final indictment to be heard was that of Alice Nutter, the ageing wife of a gentleman farmer, whose life at Roughlee was a far cry from that of her fellow accused over on the wilds of Pendle Hill. If the tightly packed throng who had turned up for a second day of entertainment were aghast at the sight of the poor folks as they stood in the dock, they were even more so when Alice took the stand. This was a rich woman, who owned her own land and employed her own workers. Her children were educated and self sufficient. She was well known throughout the area for her good, kind temper and an ever ready willingness to help out any who may require it. Yet here she was, filthy as the rest – although her gown was still clearly of a far superior quality to any of the others – standing before the law on charges of witchcraft. That such a thing was even a possibility sent shivers down the spines of the more affluent folk in the room, for if one such as Alice Nutter could be in this peril, surely it could happen to any one of them. Unless, of course, she really *was* a witch, in which case she had chosen her lot, and must not pay the price. Whereas one look at the others was enough to convince an onlooker of their guilt, Alice Nutter was a matter of division on the subject.

"Alice Nutter, you are charged with the murder of Henry Mitton. How do you plead?"

"Not guilty!"

Potts tutted to himself in the corner as he scribbled down the same words he had written repeatedly over the two day Assizes. Not one of them had entered a guilty plea, despite the evidence here presented against them. He could hardly see what they had to gain from refusing to admit their crimes. Still, he did his duty, recording their answer on paper as public record. History, not he, would judge these people. No, he thought to himself, *God* will judge them a whole lot sooner than that. He looked at Alice with a scrutinizing eye. How the mighty had fallen.

The Device Child again took the stand, as she had against each of the accused so far, and gave yet another detailed account of the evil-doings of the folks amongst whom she had been raised.

"What was Mr Mitton's crime?" Nowell asked the youngster, "for which your mother saw it fit for him to lose his life?"

"Wouldn't give 'er a penny, so he wouldn't Sir" Jennet answered confidently.

"Who was with your mother, when they set about the killing of this man?"

"There were three of 'em there, Sir" she smiled, "my Ma, my Gramma, and my Gramma's friend".

"And they were all involved?"

"Aye Sir. All did their part in th' castin' o' th' charm Sir. They had clay, Sir, and said some odd words. I dint know what they be meanin', and I fair dint like th' sound of 'em. Scared me, so they did".

"Jennet", Nowell soothed. "Do you know the name of this third woman, the friend of your Grandmother's?"

"Nutter, Sir." she grinned. "Alice Nutter".

"Tell me, Jennet. This Alice Nutter, was she present in your house on Good Friday past. At the meet, with the others you have told us about?"

"Aye, Sir. She was!"

"Jennet" Altham interjected, seemingly unconvinced by the child's testimony. "At this meeting, was there a John Bulcock present?"

"Sir, you know there was".

"An Alice Grey?"

"Aye, Sir"

"Was there an Isabel Roby present?"

Jennet shook her head. Altham tried one last time to trap the child into false witness.

"How about a..." he pretended to look down at his papers as though reading the name. "A Johan a Style?"

"Never heard o' no one by that name, Sir" she replied, after a moment's contemplation. Altham was satisfied.

"Could you show us who this Alice Nutter is?" Nowell continued baiting his young charge.

Without a seconds hesitation, Jennet Device was off the table and headed into the open courtroom. The crowd craned their necks as far as they could to see where she was going. Quick as a spooked hare, she made her way over to the accused – Alice having been directed back to her seat before the child's testimony began – and leaned beneath the bar, grabbing the woman's hand in hers and holding it high.

"This is Alice Nutter, Sir" she shouted, her voice echoing across the room.

Nowell nodded for her to release the hand, which she did, skipping merrily back to the magistrate without a care in the world. Alice showed no reaction. Nowell indicated that his examination was complete. Bromley leaned forward, thanked the child for her service, and dismissed her from the court. She made her exit loftily past the bench, towards the gentlewoman waiting at the rear of the room who took her by the hand. On reaching the door, she turned back to look at Roger Nowell, who nodded gravely in her direction before throwing her a quick wink in acknowledgement. The child had done him well.

All that was left now was to deliver the verdicts on the remaining prisoners. As had happened on the previous day, the jury were dismissed to examine and discuss what they had seen and heard that day, while the accused were left in the dock to wait, wonder and worry about what came next. All too soon, the decision was made. Katherine Hewitt, Alice Nutter, Anne Redfern, John and Jane Bulcock were all found guilty. Nowell sat back in his chair. His work was done. He would await his reward.

38

It was early the next morning that the guards came for them.

One by one, the prisoners were hauled up the steps of the Well Tower Dungeon for the final time, and thrown out into the courtyard to await their next journey. Covell was already there, anxious to rid himself of his now infamous charges. Dressed in his full warden's attire, he marched up and down before the decrepit gaggle of people, a menacing sneer across his smug, plump face. Eventually he spoke.

"May God have mercy upon your wretched souls" was all he said.

A cart pulled into the courtyard, its wheels clattering and jolting over the cobblestones. Covell exchanged words with the austere looking man in the driver's seat before motioning to the guards to act. Without hesitation, Alice Nutter and Old Chattox were pulled towards the vehicle, Anne Redfern watched in dismay as her mother was hoisted up and seated, iron chains wrapped around her feet and fastened securely to a bar across the centre. With a cry she attempted to rush forwards, her movement halted by the guard immediately behind her, who pulled her forcefully back into position. Restrained, she could only watch as the two elderly women were spirited away, through the gatehouse, and into the distance. Anne gazed after them, her mind whirring with the belief that that might well be the last time she would ever set eyes on her mother. There had been no time for goodbyes.

With Chattox and Alice gone, the remaining eight silently awaited their own transportation, each one of them flanked by the guard charged with their deliverance, until the sound of thundering wheels once more travelled up the hill. Three carts this time; the prisoners were separated into groups as they pulled to a stop, the horses bobbing their heads up and down as they danced on the spot. Soon, they settled down, poking their nosing around the cobbles as though looking for treasure. A whip cracked, sharp and loud. Alison jumped as the noise seared through her, every nerve in her body startled by the sudden attack. Rapidly the two lines were shepherded up onto the carts, chained to the bar as were the ones who had already begun their journey, and ordered to sit. Each dutifully obeyed. When the final passenger was ready, the convoy rattled slowly out of the courtyard, through the gate house, and away from the towering walls of Lancaster Castle, Covell in the front, the condemned following behind. Like lambs heading out to slaughter. They hit a bump in the road as they approached Moor Lane; Alison put her hand onto the seat to steady herself, her fingers slipping down between the two pieces of wood. Intrigued, she inspected the space, a feeling of nausea washing over her as she realised that the rough material beneath her bottom was not covering the usual bench of a cart at all. It was a coffin. Staring straight ahead at the countryside around her, she just hoped it was empty.

On they rattled through the streets of Lancaster, crowds gathering at the sides of the road to cheer on the macabre procession. Every so often something would be thrown towards the cart, usually missing the target by a good way, although one item did make contact with Anne Redfern's right cheek, leaving a slimy red streak down her skin and a hurt look in her dull grey eyes. She tried desperately not to react. Alison reached out and laid her hand gently on that of the older woman and they remained in that position, neither once looking at each other, until they reached a public house on the corner of Brewery Lane. Each passenger was then lifted from the cart and led towards the door; Alison shuddered as she edged her way past the shiny gold lion on the wall that reared up onto its hind legs as though ready to attack. She had heard of lions – they were huge, frightening creatures, with a loud roar, sharp teeth and a terrible hunger that made them eat anything that crossed their path – but she had never seen one, and had little desire to do so. Not that that was likely now.

The inn was dark inside, with wooden panels on all the walls that only served to enhance the dismal atmosphere of the place. People sat on benches, their drinks resting on solid oak tables as they looked upon the new arrivals and whispered between themselves, not always discreetly. Every head in the place turned to look at them as they were set in place at a long piece of furniture in the centre of the room and each handed a mug of lukewarm ale by a miserable looking man with a swollen stomach and a rather large wart on the side of his nose. Alison could feel their stares tingle on her skin. These people knew who she was, who they all were, and where they were headed. She felt like a prized lamb on market day.

Covell received his tankard with a handshake and raised his glass with a grisly smile.

"Your last drink" he boomed, ensuring that everyone in the vicinity heard his words. Alison stared at her mug. She didn't want to drink her portion. What did it matter if she should go to her death thirsty or watered? What difference would it make? She watched as the others drank their fill, before emptying the contents down her sore, dry throat. It had been a long time since she had tasted anything quite so satisfying, so fresh. She licked her cracked lips as though trying to savour the taste. They felt rough and brittle, and they stung at their contact with the ale. Alison sighed and stared down at her arms. She could barely pinch herself now, so wasted and thin was her skin that there was no flesh to grip. Her legs were faring no better. The skin she still possessed was a combination of yellow and dirty black colours and her eyes were struggling to adjust to being readmitted to daylight, giving her sharp pains at every available opportunity. She was beginning to grow tired of her own body.

They spent somewhere around an hour in the Golden Lion while each of the condemned were allowed to finish their beverage, and Mr Covell was busied in filling his own stomach, and regaling the innkeeper with exaggerated tales of witches and evil spirits, and how he was taking some of these abominable characters to meet their maker. He made no attempt to disguise his contempt for his travelling companions, nor to prevent them from hearing his words. Alison hated him more with every passing minute, and found herself imagining his demise in the most gruesome of fashions. If she had true magic, that man would have been dealt with a good while earlier. But she had no such powers, and she was unable to do anything more than sit and wait. She would be free of him soon. She would be free of all of it. With that there could be no doubt; Alison Device had accepted her fate.

39

By the time the cortège reached the foot of the moorland hill, the place was already overrun with people. Indeed it was so busy that there was barely a patch of ground to be seen for the majority of the way up to the summit. The air was buzzing with anticipation and excitement. Children ran between groups, playing tag or some other chasing games, their giggles echoing in the morning breeze. A crow circled overhead, adding it's voice to the bubbling fervour as it winged its way over the peak and into the distance. It was as though the whole of Lancashire was present in the place, at that moment, their common interest lying solely in the desire to watch people die.

The carts rumbled up the gravel pathway, which the guards had taken great pains to ensure was free of the crowd, the driver having slowed the horses in order to give the spectators the best possible view of the condemned. There was nothing thrown this time, but the staring, pointing and audible jeering was enough to make Alison's eyes brim with tears. Perhaps she should have been used to it by now; people had been treating her like vermin since she was old enough to remember – possibly even longer than that – yet there was something different about that morning. Something sinister, hateful even. Something that made her want to rip her heart out and show them that she was just the same as them. Just a person. A human. But of course, they had been told otherwise. To them, she – they – were monsters.

A drum began its doleful sound from somewhere above them, marking their ascent up the gradual incline of the hill. At that moment the wind picked up its pace, her whole body shivering in its wake as it danced briskly across the open moor. And then she saw it; the huge wooden structure that was to be her end.

It rose into the air like a giant fireplace, perhaps three times her height and wider still. From the top piece of wood dangled five lengths of what she assumed to be rope, each pulled round into a broad loop and finished off with a large knot where it connected to the main thread. They swayed in the breeze as though inviting her to step nearer. A second, identical construction stood a little to the right. Alison turned her head away; she could not bear to look at them any longer.

Within seconds, the carts were stopped beneath the two sets of gallows, where a portly man in a long black robe was awaiting their arrival. He stalked the ground in front like a predator searching for its kill, a heavy book nestled beneath his arm as he eyed up his victims. Alison felt his eyes upon her, and met him with a steely look of her own. This man was about to send her to meet her Maker; he was not going to do it until he had looked her in the eye. She was determined. She had nothing left to lose.

She heard her guard whisper something in her ear, something that she couldn't quite decipher through the hissing and jeering that hurtled through the air, penetrating her senses like a knife through butter. She heard it a second time. Again it failed to register. Suddenly she felt herself being pulled upwards, her agile young gaoler having hoisted himself up onto the vehicle, and made to stand on her aching feet. The material on which they had been seated was whipped from beneath them, revealing the coffins below to the salivating crowd, before each of the ten were pushed into climbing upon them, the wood smooth and cold against their skin. They stood, lined up across the two carts like a morbid theatre attraction, staring out over the vast Lancashire countryside, while the mob heckled and jeered below, every insult hurled venomously in their direction. The atmosphere was beginning to change.

The man with the book once more took the stage, his eyes now fixed on his audience rather than the unfortunate subjects of his rantings, the book now resting firmly in his right hand.

"These *people* behind me" he began, spitting the word out in sheer disgust.

"These *people* have been judged to be in violation of God's Word in the most *vile,* the most *foul,* the most *wicked* ways possible".

The mob roared below.

"They have been convicted and condemned by both God and the Law, and will today, here, meet that judgement".

He paused to allow more hissing and taunting to float up the hillside.

"Mr Covell, who are these people?"

Covell stepped forwards his chest inflated by a sense of importance. Walking across the facade of the two structures, he slowly identified cach of the prisoners, pointing each one out to the fascinated onlookers.

"Anne Whittle, otherwise known as Old Chattox".

Someone snorted loudly and spat at the ground.

"Elizabeth Device, daughter of the infamous Old Demdike".

"Witch" came a cry from somewhere beyond.

"James Device, her son".

"Devil's spawn" was heard in the air.

"Katherine Hewitt"

More hissing.

"Anne Redfern, daughter of Old Chattox".

With each name, Covell waited for the inevitable reaction. He was clearly enjoying his moment. He moved on to the second set of gallows.

"Jane Bulcock".

"John Bulcock".

"Isabel Robey".

The assemblage murmured amongst themselves. They were acquainted with the other nine folks on the carts, but this Isabel Robey was a stranger to them. They recognised neither face nor name. Alison cast a glance sideways at her elderly counterpart; the only non-Pendle one amongst them. Isabel offered her a weak, defeated smile.

Looking out over the green fields beyond, Isabel longed to see her home again; that small hamlet of Windle in which she had been born and raised. She caught sight of her god-daughter in the gathering, tears clearly evident in her dark eyes, her husband standing calmly by her side. Isabel half snarled at the sight of him – the man who had accused her, the man who had led her to this place. She had never liked him, much less approved of his match with her beloved Mary, and now, here she was, condemned by his words. Mary bowed her head to avoid eye contact. Her husband smirked as he considered the culmination of his work. Covell continued the line-up.

"Alice Nutter".

Audible gasps flew through the air like the current of a fast flowing river. Alice Nutter, the kindly old lady of Crowtrees Farm, the wealthy, devout Catholic gentry woman whose benevolence was more than well know in the area, now standing beneath her death rope alongside some of the basest human beings on earth. Mrs Nutter, a witch? How could this be true? There must have been some kind of mistake. A big mistake. The people looked around the hillside, searching for a glimpse of one of the Nutter children who would surely step forward in defence of their mother. Not one of them were to be seen. Alice too, seemed to be scanning the group. On finding nothing, she heaved a heavy sigh and dropped her head. She was not too surprised – they had been absent throughout the duration of the trial, there was little use in thinking they would come to her now. Yet she had hoped, and had been disappointed. Her children had forsaken her.

Nowell regarded the introductions with an air of satisfaction. He had chosen his position carefully to ensure the best view of the proceedings possible, and also to gage the reactions of the spectators at every turn. His efforts proved worthwhile. Every jeer, every hiss confirmed his vivid belief that he had been more than vindicated in his ardent pursuit of justice. These people believed in witchcraft, feared it, and wanted it eradicated. He had saved them from the evil at work around them. There was no doubt in his mind; he, Roger Nowell, was the Saviour of Pendle Forest.

Covell continued, naming the last of the wretches beneath the gallows, the one who had unwittingly brought about the entire sorry proceedings that were now coming to fruition.

"Alison Device".

More cries of 'witch' rose from below. Alison tried hard to show no reaction, despite the fact that her heart was beating like a caged bird within her chest and her skin was seemingly crawling over her bones. There were people she knew or had known, there were complete strangers who had heard frightening stories about happenings up on the big hill, there were people who had come from miles away to participate in the day's entertainment. They were all so ready to label her a witch, a devil; to watch her hang for her perceived crimes, real or otherwise. They didn't care whether she were truly guilty, nor were they interested in her upbringing and poverty. She was a witch. Witches must die. And that was that. At that moment, with every fibre of her entire being, she hated each and every one of them.

The presence of Abraham Lawe loomed large in the cluster as he stood almost at the centre front. With his thick arms crossed squarely across his chest, he cut an imposing figure, his features distorted with the bitterness and contempt that he clearly felt towards these now denounced demons. The girl had showed remorse, that much was true, yet the continuing struggles of his ailing father rendered Abraham incapable of any display of clemency towards the child who had maimed him. John Lawe had refused to attend the execution, just as he had the trial, leaving Abraham feeling that it was his duty to ensure that justice was done. The time was fast approaching. There would be no mercy here.

Somewhere to her left she heard her mother shriek into the air. Startled, Alison turned to see the woman pointing a thin, bony finger out towards before her, her breathing becoming increasingly more agitated with every second. Alison looked to decipher what had affected her so; and there she was, little Jennet Device, standing hand in hand with Nowell's wife, her neatly styled brown hair blowing innocently in the wind. Alison squinted to get a better look at her younger sibling. Dressed in a fine yellow dress and little fur coat, she no longer looked like the Jennet that she knew, in her ragged smock and bare feet, but more like the well heeled daughter of a monied family on an August outing. She was clean and nourished, and clearly well cared for. Alison felt a tiny prick of jealousy at her sister's new life, until the strangled, incoherence of her mother reminded her that such changes had been wrought through lies and betrayal. Her eyes narrowed as she glared at the child, who held the woman's hand all the more tightly and half turned away from the attention. Alison maintained the glare. The little rat was not in the least bit sorry.

The priest once more took the stage, delivering a loud lecture on evil and witchcraft, the justice of the Lord and the punishment of the wicked. The prisoners offered nothing in response. The time for that had long since passed, if it had ever been there at all. After what felt to be an age, he finally completed his tirade and rejoined the crowd, his chest expanded in both satisfaction and self righteousness. His work was done. He was ready.

The invisible drumming once more began its mournful beat; slow and death like in its tone as it hung thickly in the air. A bird squawked and took flight. The crowd surged forward, jostling for the best viewpoint as each of the ten guards boarded the carts, placing the huge, thick ropes round the necks of their charges and tightening the knots. Alison's man placed his hand on her shoulder. She turned; he was so close to her that she could feel his breath on her skin.

"Soon be over, Miss" he whispered, a note of melancholy in his voice. "Be strong".

And with that he was gone. Alison swallowed hard, the first tender contact she had received in a long time weighing lightly on the shoulder he had just touched as he and the other guards discharged their duties. The beat rumbled into a thunderous roll, the excitement of the spectators rising alongside it, before levelling once more into the series of slow, steady strikes. Alison did not notice the two drivers taking their positions behind the horses, so desperately was she attempting to think of the words of the old prayers that her Grand mother had once taught her. She could hear Alice Nutter reciting similar ones at her side, but she could not place the words in her memory. She wished she had paid more attention.

Another ominous rolling of batons against drum roared. Alison felt the cart wobble beneath her, shifting her feet to gain a better foothold on the coffin below. Suddenly, there was a whipping noise and the horses began to move. The carts pulled away simultaneously, dropping the prisoners to the mercy of the ropes around their necks. The air was filled with the sounds of gasping and choking, and the kicking of feet as they tried to find solid ground. The audience cheered in excitement. Alison clawed at her neck as the noose burrowed into her flesh, her dirt stained fingers making no impression upon the offending object. Her throat tightened and her eyes felt as though the might explode from their sockets at any moment. Her vision blurred, yet she could just make out an outline in the distance. She tried to make out what it was; it didn't look to be human for it was much lower to the ground even than a child, and it appeared to walk on four feet rather than two. As it zoomed closer into view, it began to focus. It was a dog. A huge, black dog that she was certain that she had seen somewhere before. It seated itself at the front of the crowd, looking up at her with bright, red eyes that shone through the encroaching blackness. It was the same dog that had been with her at Colne Field on the morning that she had met the peddler man, the morning that everything had started to go wrong. The dog bared its teeth in what looked like an enormous grin before turning and running off down the hillside and into the distance. Finally, everything went black.

Bodies swayed silently in the breeze. There was no more movement. No more struggling. No more life. The priest boomed something about this being the punishment of all of God's enemies and the crowd responded with cries of "Long Live King James" and "God Save the King. Ladders were quickly erected at the gallows, the corpses were removed and taken to the carts on which they had arrived some time earlier. Placed one by one in the wooden coffins, they were driven slowly away in the direction of the ancient castle that had been their home for the previous few months. The crowd began to disperse. The spectacle was over.

40

Roger Nowell left Gallows Hill that day with a strange feeling brewing in his stomach. He had done the King's work, he knew that, and the King had demanded that all witches, all witch*craft* must be dealt with swiftly and decisively. He had succeeded in that, he was in no doubt. Yet something was bothering him. An ominous sensation that burned within him, with little indication as to what its cause might be. Seated in the carriage that would take him back to Read Hall, he regarded the child alongside him, his new charge that he had rescued from that future of deprivation and evil she would surely have grown up in within her own family. The child, Jennet, slumbered peacefully on the arm of her new mother, her freckled face showing the faintest indication of the silent tears she had shed as she watched her entire family hang on the Lancashire moor. He hadn't seen her cry, but then he had taken little notice of her that morning, so engaged was he in the culmination of his greatest work to date. He had resigned the child to the care and concern of his wife, who he presumed had wiped her tears and told her of the life that was to come. Nowell had never considered that the experience would upset the child, so confident and assured she was that her family were evil and deserved their fate. Now, in the comfort of that carriage, he could see that she had, indeed been affected by what she had just witnessed. That she was – rather than being the most important witness and linchpin of his ardent campaign – a small, helpless child who had only wanted to please him, who had wanted to punish her kin in some way for her mean existence with little understanding of the consequences of her words. Now she was an orphan. Alone in the world, save for himself and his family. Traumatised by watching the deaths of everyone she had ever had. The folks of Pendle knew of her involvement in the trial. Belief in witches was one thing, but could he be sure of the response the child would get with the outcome. She could be ostracised, blamed, hated even. He could not imagine any family in the area willing to take in such a seemingly ungrateful, scheming little girl. Nowell knew what he must do. Banishing all previous thoughts of placing the child into a new, unfamiliar family, he realised that he had created a perceived monster, and now he must deal with it. History would judge them both. Little Jennet Device was now his responsibility. Forever.

41

A state of calm had once more begun to settle over Pendle Forest in the weeks and months following the events on Gallows Hill. The world continued in its eternal cycle; night turned to day, and day back to night, Autumn gave way to the colder temperatures and winds of Winter and everyday life went on much as it always had for the remaining residents of the villages and farms that made up the land surrounding the now infamous great hill. After a while all talk of magic and witches subsided as other gossip began to remove it as the main topic of conversation. Some folks simply preferred the subject to go away for fear of more accusations being made, and this time against themselves or their kin. Fear remained prevalent, but now it was silent, choosing instead to hide inside homes and families rather than out in the open. In short, nobody wanted to risk being next.

Sitting at the high wooden desk in his study, one man contemplated the fate of the witches of Pendle, and what might come of their stories. Such a large conviction for witchcraft – so many people in one place, at one time – was unheard of and was, as such, a huge story throughout the land. One that may just persuade people that magic was not a path down which they should travel. A story that should be remembered for years to come. Besides, Mr Nowell had put so much effort into bringing these people to justice in the name of the King, he deserved to be acknowledged for his diligence and hard work, rather than it all be forgotten with the passage of time and person. That could not be allowed to happen. He, Thomas Potts, would not allow it.

Removing the heavy pile of papers from its case, he quietly perused the first page for a moment as the idea formed in his mind. Presently, he set the hand written material to one side, pulled out a fresh stack from the drawer beside his right knee and manoeuvred his chair as close to the desk as he could get it.

So he began.

On the sixteenth day of November, he set down his quill for the final time, a feeling of accomplishment ebbing through him as he surveyed the completed manuscript before him. Hours of testimony, interrogation and trial now formed a tome of which he was proud, and he was certain that Mr Nowell and others would share his satisfaction that the now locally infamous Pendle Witch trials and convictions would become more widely known. Nowell would become legendary as a man who would not tolerate evil in his midst. The King would revel in the knowledge that his policies were being successfully carried out. The judges could rest knowing that justice had won. The witches themselves would live on in history as a lesson in behaviour and the importance of reputation. And he, Thomas Potts would be the man whose writings would bring it all together in this piece of work – and perhaps make some money out of it at the same time. A winning situation for all, he thought to himself stroking his beard and imagining what the future might hold. As the day began to draw to a murky close, he found another sheet, held out his quill for a moment as though considering carefully his next words, before scribbling across the centre of the paper, in the neatest handwriting he could produce.

The Wonderfull Discoverie of

Witches in the Countie of

Lancaster.

By Thomas Potts, Esquire.

And with that, his work was done. Pendle Forest had expunged its demons; had rid itself of the Devil and his minions, and their evil doings forever. Now, its people could live in peace and security that God was, indeed, still with them. It was over.

The End

Particular thanks are expressed to the following authors and works, which have provided much of the information and inspiration needed to complete this work.

Bennet, W *The Pendle Witches*
             Lancashire County Books,
             1993

Clayton, J A *The Lancashire Witch Conspiracy: A History of Pendle Forest and the Pendle Witch Trials*
             Second Edition
             Barrowford Press, 2007

Poole, R (Ed) *The Lancashire Witches*
                  Histories and Stories
             Manchester University Press
             2002

Printed in Great Britain
by Amazon